THE DAY OF THE OWL

LEONARDO SCIASCIA was born in Sicily in 1912. He was a renowned Italian novelist and essayist, as well as a polemical and outspoken political commentator who, like many of the protagonists in his novels, challenged the entrenched corruption in the government of his day. He has been described by Gore Vidal as one of the greatest modern writers. He died in 1989.

THE DAY OF THE OWL

Leonardo Sciascia

Translated from the Italian by

ARCHIBALD COLQUHOUN &

ARTHUR OLIVER

GRANTA

Granta Publications, 12 Addison Avenue, London W11 4QR

First published in Great Britain by Granta Books 2001
This edition published by Granta Books 2013
Originally published in Italian as *Il Giorno della Civetta*, copyright
© 1961 by Giulio Einaudi Editore. English translation copyright
© 1963 by Jonathan Cape, Ltd. Translated from the Italian by
Archibald Colquhoun and Arthur Oliver

A CIP catalogue record for this book
is available from the British Library.

1 3 5 7 9 10 8 6 4 2

ISBN 978 1 84708 925 0

Printed and bound by CPI Group (UK) Ltd, Croydon, CR0 4YY

MIX
Paper from
responsible sources
FSC® C020471

THE DAY OF THE OWL

THE bus was just about to leave, amid rumbles and sudden hiccups and rattles. The square was silent in the grey of dawn; wisps of cloud swirled round the belfry of the church. The only sound, apart from the rumbling of the bus, was a voice, wheedling, ironic, of a fritter-seller; fritters, hot fritters. The conductor slammed the door, and with a clank of scrap-metal the bus moved off. His last glance round the square caught sight of a man in a dark suit running towards the bus.

'Hold it a minute,' said the conductor to the driver, opening the door with the bus still in motion. Two ear-splitting shots rang out. For a second the man in the dark suit, who was just about to jump on the running-board, hung suspended in mid-air as if some invisible hand were hauling him up by the hair. Then his brief-case dropped from his hand and very slowly he slumped down on top of it.

The conductor swore; his face was the colour of sulphur; he was shaking. The fritter-seller, who was only three yards from the fallen man, sidled off with a crab-like motion towards the door of the church. In the bus no one moved; the driver sat, as if turned to stone, his right hand on the brake, his left on the steering-wheel. The conductor looked round the passengers' faces, which were blank as the blinds.

'They've killed him,' he said; he took off his cap, swore again, and began frantically running his fingers through his hair.

'The carabinieri,' said the driver, 'we must get the carabinieri.'

He got up and opened the other door. 'I'll go,' he said to the conductor.

The conductor looked at the dead man and then at the passengers. These included some women, old women who brought heavy sacks of white cloth and baskets full of eggs every morning; their clothes smelled of forage, manure and wood smoke; usually they grumbled and swore, now they sat mute, their faces as if disinterred from the silence of centuries.

'Who is it?' asked the conductor, pointing at the body. No one answered. The conductor cursed. Among passengers of that route he was famous for his highly skilled blaspheming. The company had already threatened to fire him, since he never bothered to control himself even when there were nuns or priests on the bus. He was from the province of Syracuse and had had little to do with violent death: a soft province, Syracuse. So now he swore all the more furiously.

The carabinieri arrived; the sergeant-major, with a black stubble and in a black temper from being woken, stirred the passengers' apathy like an alarm-clock: in the wake of the conductor they began to get out through the door left open by the driver.

With seeming nonchalance, looking around as if they were trying to gauge the proper distance from which to admire the belfry, they drifted off towards the sides of the square and, after a last look around, scuttled into alley-ways.

The sergeant-major and his men did not notice this gradual exodus. Now about fifty people were around the dead man: men from a public works training centre who were only too delighted to have found such an absorbing topic of conversation to while away their eight hours of idleness. The sergeant-major ordered his men to clear the square and get the passengers back on to the bus. The carabinieri began pushing sightseers back towards the streets leading off the square, asking passengers to take their seats on the bus again. When the square was empty, so was the bus. Only the driver and the conductor remained.

'What?' said the sergeant-major to the driver. 'No passengers today?'

'Yes, some,' replied the driver with an absent-minded look.

'Some,' said the sergeant-major, 'means four, five or six ... I've never seen this bus leave with an empty seat.'

'How should I know?' said the driver, exhausted from straining his memory. 'How should I know? I said "some" just like that. More than five or six though. Maybe more; maybe the bus was full. I never look to see who's there. I just get into my seat and off we go. The road's the only thing I look at; that's what I'm paid for ... to look at the road.'

The sergeant-major rubbed his chin with a hand taut with irritation. 'I get it,' he said, 'you just look at the road.' He rounded savagely on the conductor. 'But you, you tear off the tickets, take money, give change. You count the people and look at their faces ... and if you don't want me to make you remember 'em in the guard-room, you're going to tell me now who was on that bus! At least ten names ... You've been on this run for the last three years, and for the last three years I've seen you every evening in the Café Italia. You know this town better than I do ... '

'Nobody could know the town better than you do,' said the conductor with a smile, as though shrugging off a compliment.

'All right, then,' said the sergeant-major, sneering, 'first me, then you … But I wasn't on the bus or I'd remember every passenger one by one. So it's up to you. Ten names at least.'

'I can't remember,' said the conductor, 'by my mother's soul I can't remember. Just now I can't remember a thing. It all seems a dream.'

'I'll wake you up,' raged the sergeant-major, 'I'll wake you up with a couple of years inside … ' He broke off to go and meet the police magistrate who had just arrived. While making his report on the identity of the dead man and the flight of the passengers, the sergeant-major looked at the bus. As he looked, he had an impression that something was not quite right or was missing, as when something in our daily routine is unexpectedly missing, which the senses perceive from force of habit but the mind does not quite apprehend; even so its absence provokes an empty feeling of discomfort, a vague exasperation as from a flickering light-bulb. Then, suddenly, what we are looking for dawns on us.

'There's something missing,' said the sergeant-major to Carabiniere Sposito, who being a qualified accountant was a pillar of the Carabinieri Station of S., 'there's something or someone missing.'

'The fritter-seller,' said Carabiniere Sposito.

'The fritter-seller, by God!' The sergeant-major exulted, thinking: 'An accountant's diploma means something.'

A carabiniere was sent off at the double to pick up the

fritter-seller. He knew where to find the man, who, after the departure of the first bus, usually went to sell his wares at the entrance of the elementary schools. Ten minutes later the sergeant-major had the vender of fritters in front of him. The man's expression was that of a man roused from innocent slumber.

'Was he there?' the sergeant-major asked the conductor.

'He was,' answered the conductor gazing at his shoe.

'Well now,' said the sergeant-major with paternal kindness, 'this morning, as usual, you came to sell your fritters here ... As usual, at the first bus for Palermo ... '

'I've my licence,' said the fritter-seller.

'I know,' said the sergeant-major, raising his eyes to heaven, imploring patience. 'I know and I'm not thinking about your licence. I want to know only one thing, and, if you tell me, you can go off at once and sell your fritters to the kids: who fired the shots?'

'Why,' asked the fritter-seller, astonished and inquisitive, 'has there been shooting?'

* * *

'Yes, at half past six. From the corner of Via Cavour. A double dose of *lupara** probably from a twelve-bore, maybe from a sawn-off shotgun ... Nobody on the bus saw a thing. A hell of a job to find out who *was* on the bus. When I got there they had all made off. A man who sells fritters remembered – after a couple of hours – seeing something like a sack of coal. He's made a vow of

Lupara literally 'wolf-shot'. A cartridge loaded with five or seven ball-bearings used for mafia killings. (Tr.)

half a peck of chick-peas to Santa Fara because by a miracle he didn't get some of the lead, he says, standing as near as he was to the target ... The conductor didn't even see the sack of coal ... The passengers, those sitting on the right-hand side, say the windows were so steamy they looked like frosted glass. Maybe true ... Yes, head of a co-operative building company, a small one which seems never to have taken on contracts for more than twenty million lire ... small building lots, workers' houses, drains, secondary roads ... Salvatore Colasberna, Co-la-sbe-rna. Used to be a bricklayer. Ten years ago he formed the company with two of his brothers and four or five local bricklayers; he was in charge of the work, though a surveyor figured as director, and used to keep the accounts. They got along as best they could. He and his associates were content with a small profit, as though they were working for wages ... No, it seems they didn't do the sort of job that gets washed away by the first shower of rain ... I've seen a farm building, brand new, caved in like a cardboard box because a cow rubbed against it ... No, built by the Smiroldi company, big building contractors. A farm building smashed by a cow! ... Colasberna, they tell me, used to do a solid job. There's the Via Madonna di Fatima here, made by his outfit, which hasn't sunk a centimetre, in spite of all the trucks that use it; while other streets, made by much bigger contractors, look like a camel's back after only a year ... Had he a criminal record? Yes, in nineteen forty ... here we are, in nineteen forty, the third of November, nineteen forty ... He was travelling on a bus – he doesn't seem to have much luck with buses – and people were discussing the war we had just declared on Greece;

14

someone said: "We'll suck it dry in a fortnight" – he meant Greece. Colasberna said: "What is *it*? An egg?" There was a Blackshirt on the bus who reported him ... What? ... Sorry, you asked me if he had a criminal record and I, with the file in front of me, say he had ... All right, then, he hadn't a criminal record ... Me? ... A Fascist? When I see fasces I touch wood ... Yes, sir. Yours to command.'

He replaced the telephone on its hook with the delicacy of exasperation and wiped his forehead with his handkerchief. 'This one's been a partisan,' he said. 'I would have the luck to hit on someone who's been a partisan!'

*　　*　　*

The two surviving Colasberna brothers and the other members of the Santa Fara Co-operative Building Society were waiting for the captain to arrive. They were all sitting in a row, dressed in black; the brothers had black woollen shawls over their shoulders, and bloodshot eyes; they were unshaven in sign of mourning. Motionless they sat in the waiting-room of the Carabinieri Station of S., their eyes riveted to a coloured target painted on the wall with the ironic wording: UNLOAD FIREARMS HERE. They felt an overwhelming shame at being in such a place and at having to wait. Compared to shame, death is nothing.

Sitting apart from them, perched on the edge of her chair, was a young woman. She had come in after them and wanted to see the sergeant-major, so she told the orderly. The reply was that the sergeant-major was busy and the captain was on his way. 'I'll wait,' she said, and

15

sat on the edge of her chair, fidgeting with her fingers so that it made the others nervy to look at her. They knew her by sight; she was the wife of a tree-pruner from another village who had come from near-by B. to settle down in S. after the war, married here, and now in this poverty-stricken place – what with his wife's dowry and his job – was considered well-off.

'She's had a row with her husband and has come to make a charge,' thought the members of the Santa Fara Co-operative Society, and the thought helped take their minds off that burning shame of theirs.

There came a sound of a car pulling up in the court-yard, and of the engine cutting off, then the click of heels down the passage. Into the waiting-room came the captain, for whom the warrant-officer opened the door of his own office with a salute so stiff and a head held so high that he seemed to be inspecting the ceiling. The captain was young, tall and fair-skinned. At his first words the Santa Fara members thought, with a mixture of relief and scorn, 'A mainlander.' Mainlanders are decent enough but just don't understand things.

Again they sat down in a row in front of the sergeant-major's desk. The captain sat in the desk-chair with the sergeant-major standing beside him, and on the other side, crouched over the typewriter, sat Carabiniere Sposito. Sposito had a baby face, but the brothers Colasberna and their associates were in holy terror of his presence, the terror of a merciless inquisition, of the black seed of the written word. 'White soil, black seed. Beware of the man who sows it. He never forgets,' says the proverb.

The captain offered his condolences and apologized for

summoning them to the barracks and for keeping them waiting. Again they thought: 'A mainlander; they're polite, mainlanders,' but they still kept a wary eye on Carabiniere Sposito whose hands were lightly poised over the keyboard of the typewriter, tense and silent as a hunter lying in wait for a hare in the moonlight, his finger on the trigger.

'It's odd,' said the captain, as though continuing an interrupted discussion, 'how people in this part of the world let themselves go in anonymous letters. No one talks, but luckily for us – I mean us carabinieri, of course – everyone writes. They may forget to sign, but they do write. After every murder, every hold-up, there are a dozen anonymous letters on my desk. Even after a family row or a fraudulent bankruptcy they write. And as for my men's love-affairs ... ' He smiled at his sergeant-major, and the Santa Fara members thought he might be alluding to the fact that Carabiniere Savarino was having an affair with the daughter of Palazzolo the tobacconist, as was known in the whole town where an early posting for Savarino was expected.

'As for the Colasberna case,' went on the captain, 'I've already had five anonymous letters; quite a crop for something that only happened the day before yesterday – and there'll be more to come. One nameless correspondent says that Colasberna was killed out of jealousy and gives the name of the jealous husband ... '

'Nonsense,' said Giuseppe Colasberna.

'I agree,' said the captain and went on: 'According to another he was killed by mistake, because he happened to resemble a man called Perricone, who – my anonymous informer says – deserves what's soon coming to him.'

'That might be,' said Giuseppe Colasberna.

'No, it mightn't,' said the captain, 'because the Perricone mentioned in the letter got a passport a couple of weeks ago and right now happens to be in Liège, Belgium. You didn't know that, maybe; certainly the writer of the letter didn't; but the fact could hardly have escaped the notice of anyone intending to bump him off ... I won't waste your time with other even more ridiculous information, but there is one aspect of the case to which I would ask you to give serious thought ... In my opinion, it might be the right track. I mean your own work, competition, contracts. That's where we should start.'

Another quick glance of consultation. 'That can't be,' said Giuseppe Colasberna.

'Oh, yes, it can,' said the captain, 'and I'll tell you exactly how and why. Apart from your particular case, I've a great deal of inside information on the contracting business, only hearsay, unfortunately, but if I had proof ... Well now, let's just suppose that in this district, in this province, there are ten contracting firms operating. Each firm has its own machinery and materials, that lie by the roadside or on the building site at night. Machines are delicate things. All you have to do is remove a piece, even a single bolt, and it will take hours or days to get it running again. As for the materials, fuel oil, tar, timber, it's easy enough to lift those or burn them on the spot. True, there is often a hut near the machinery and materials where some workmen sleep, but that's just it; they sleep. Well now, there are other people – and you know who I mean – who never sleep. Wouldn't it be natural to turn to these people – these people who never sleep – for protection? Especially when protection has been offered you at once and, if you've been unwise enough to refuse it, something has happened to make you decide to accept it ... Of course, there are the stubborn, the people who say no they don't want it, and wouldn't accept it even with a knife at their throats. From what I can see, you're stubborn ... or perhaps only Salvatore was ... '

'This is all new to us,' said Giuseppe Colasberna, and the others, with taut faces, nodded assent.

'Maybe it is, maybe it isn't,' said the captain, 'but I haven't finished yet. Now, let's say that nine out of ten contractors accept or ask for protection. It would be a poor sort of association – and you know what association I refer to – if it were to limit itself to the functions and pay of night-watchmen. The protection offered by the association is on a much vaster scale. It obtains private contracts for you, I mean for the firms which toe the line and accept protection. It gives you valuable tips if you want to submit a tender for public works, it supports you when the final inspection comes up, it saves trouble with your workmen ... Obviously, if nine companies out of ten have accepted protection, thus forming a kind of union, the tenth which refuses is a black sheep. It can't do much harm, of course, but its very existence is a challenge and a bad example. So, by fair means or foul, it must be forced to come into the fold or be wiped out once and for all.'

Giuseppe Colasberna said: 'This is the first I've ever heard of all this,' and his brother and partners made signs of approval.

'Now, let's suppose,' went on the captain as though he

had not heard, 'that your company, the Santa Fara, is the black sheep of the district, the one that won't play ball, that submits honest tenders and competes for contracts without protection. Sometimes, especially with the system of maximum and minimum prices, it succeeds in making the winning offer simply because it has made an honest estimate ... One fine day, a person "worthy of respect", as you would say, comes to have a little talk with Salvatore Colasberna; what he says might mean anything and nothing, allusive, blurred as the back of a piece of embroidery, a tangle of knots and threads with the pattern on the other side ... Colasberna cannot or will not look at the other side and the man "worthy of respect" takes umbrage. The association moves into action; as a first warning, a small dump goes up in smoke, or something like that. Then comes a second warning; late one evening, round about eleven, as you are on your way home, a bullet just misses you ... '

The partners of the Santa Fara avoided the captain's eyes. They stared at their hands, looked up at the portrait of the Commander-in-Chief of the Carabinieri, at that of the President of the Republic and at the crucifix hanging on the wall. After a long pause, the captain struck just where they were most sensitive.

'I seem to remember something of the kind happening to your brother six months ago,' he said, 'just as he was going home, round about eleven ... Didn't it?'

'Er ... I ... I never heard about it,' stammered Giuseppe.

'They won't talk,' broke in the warrant-officer, 'even if they're picked off one by one, they still won't talk. They'd sooner get themselves killed ... '

The captain interrupted him with a gesture. 'Listen,' he said, 'there's a woman waiting out there ... '

'I'll go at once,' said the sergeant-major, rather crestfallen.

'There's no more for me to say to you,' went on the captain. 'I've already said a good deal and you have nothing to tell me. Before you go I want each one of you to write his name and surname, place and date of birth, and address on this sheet of paper.'

'I write very slowly,' said Giuseppe, and the others affirmed that they also wrote slowly and with difficulty.

'No matter,' said the captain, 'there's plenty of time.' He lit a cigarette and watched the efforts of the partners on the sheet of paper. They wrote as if the pen were as heavy as a pneumatic drill: and because of their awkwardness and shaking hands, it vibrated like one too. When they had finished, he rang for the orderly, who came in with the sergeant-major.

'Show these gentlemen out,' ordered the captain.

'Christ, he knows how to treat people,' thought the partners, and in their joy at having been almost spared (the 'almost' referred to those specimens of their handwriting the captain had wanted) and at having been called gentlemen by an officer of Carabinieri, they went out quite forgetful of their mourning and longing to run and skip like boys just let out of school.

Meanwhile the captain was comparing their handwriting with that of the anonymous letter. He was sure that one of them had written it and, in spite of its clumsy slope and disguise, it did not need an expert to tell by comparing it to that of the personal details on the other sheet of paper in front of him that the writer was

Giuseppe Colasberna. The clue provided by the anonymous letter was a sure one.

The sergeant-major could not understand why the captain was bothering to study that handwriting.

'It's like squeezing tripe: nothing comes out,' he said, meaning the Colasberna brothers, their partners, the town in general and Sicily as a whole.

'No, something,' replied the captain.

'Well, as long as you're happy,' thought the sergeant-major, mentally using the personal "tu". In his inner thoughts he would use it with General Lombardi himself.

'What about that woman now?' asked the captain, getting up to leave again.

'It's about her husband,' answered the sergeant-major. 'He went off into the country the day before yesterday to do some pruning and is not back yet. He must have been invited to some farmhouse party, you know, a fat lamb and lots of wine, then he probably went to sleep it off in a haystack, dead drunk ... He'll turn up this evening, I'll bet my life.'

'The day before yesterday ... If I were you I'd start looking for him,' said the captain.

'Yes, sir,' said the sergeant-major.

*   *   *

'I don't like him,' said the man in black, looking as if his teeth were on edge from eating unripe plums; his sun-baked face, alive with a peculiar intelligence, was wry with disgust. 'I don't like him at all.'

'But you didn't like the other one, the one before him,

either. Do we have to change 'em every couple of weeks?' said, with a smile, a well-dressed fair man who was sitting beside him. Both were Sicilians and differed only in physique and manners.

They were in a café in Rome, a pink, silent room with mirrors, chandeliers like great clusters of flowers and a shapely brunette cloakroom girl who looked as if she could be peeled out of her black dress like a fruit.

She shouldn't be made merely to take it off, thought both the fair man and the dark man alike, but it should be removed stitch by stitch.

'I took a dislike to that other fellow because of the fuss he made about firearm licences,' said the dark man.

'And before the firearm licences there was someone else you disliked because of the internment camp.'

'Is an internment camp a laughing matter?'

'No, no laughing matter at all, I know; but, for one reason or another, you never manage to get on with any of them.'

'But this is different. The presence of a man like him in our part of the world ought to upset you more than it does me. He was a partisan; with all the hotbed of communists we have down there, they had to send us an ex-partisan as well. No wonder our interests are going to pieces ... '

'But what evidence have you that he protects the communists?'

'I'll give you just one example. You know how badly the sulphur mines are doing at the moment. I curse the day I ever went into partnership with Scarantino in that mine. What little capital I had, my life's blood, is being sucked dry by that mine. We're ruined.'

23

'So you're ruined, then,' said the fair man, ironically incredulous.

'Well, if I'm not utterly ruined, I owe it to you. To you and the government which, one must admit, really has been taking measures over the sulphur crisis ... '

'Such measures that with the money it pays out you could pay your workers regularly and adequately without them ever going down the mine; and perhaps that would be the best solution.'

'Anyway, things are going badly. And, of course, they are going badly for everybody. Why should I be the only one to pay? The workers must pay their share as well ... They've had no wages for two weeks ... '

'Three months,' corrected the other man with a smile.

'I don't remember exactly ... Anyway, they went and held a protest meeting outside my house ... such foul language and catcalls ... they deserve to be shot ... Well, I went to complain to him and d'you know what he said to me? "Have you eaten today?" "Yes, I have," I said. "Yesterday, too?" he asked. "Yesterday, too," I said. "Is your family starving?" he asked. "No, thank the Lord," I replied. "And these people who came and made a row outside your house, have they eaten today?" I was on the point of saying: "What the hell do I care whether they have eaten or not?" but from politeness I replied: "I don't know." He said, "You ought to find out." "I've come to you," I told him, "because they are outside my house and threatening me. My wife and daughters can't even go out to go to Mass." "Oh," he said, "we'll see that they get to Mass all right. That's what we're here for ... You don't pay your workmen but we see

24

that your wife and daughters get to Mass." I'm telling you, the look on his face made my fingers itch and you know how hot-blooded I am ... '

'Now, now, now,' said the fair man in crescendo, his tone reproving the urge to violence and at the same time enjoining discretion.

'Oh, nowadays my nerves are as steady as a winch-rope. I'm not what I used to be thirty years ago. But I say: has a policeman ever dared to talk so to a man of honour before? He's a communist. Only communists talk like that.'

'Not only communists, unfortunately. We have people in the party who talk just the same ... If you knew the struggle we have, every day ... every hour ... '

'I know. They're all the same to me, communists, the lot of them.'

'They're not communists,' said the fair man, gloomily thoughtful.

'Well, if they aren't communists, why doesn't the Pope give them a little plain talk? That'd fix them.'

'It's not quite so simple ... but enough of that. To return to our little matter, what's the name of this ... communist?'

'Bellodi, I think. He commands the Carabinieri Company in C. and in three months he's already become a nuisance. Now he's poking his nose into local contracting companies ... Commendatore Zarcone is counting on you too. He said to me only the other day: "Let's hope our Honourable Member gets him sent back north to eat polenta!" '

'Dear old Zarcone!' said the Honourable Member. 'How is he?'

'He could be doing better,' said the dark man with meaning.

'We'll see that he does,' promised the Honourable Member.

*   *   *

Captain Bellodi, commanding the Carabinieri of C., sat facing the 'informer' of S. He had sent for him, with the usual precautions, to find out what the man thought about the Colasberna killing. Usually when something serious happened in the town the informer showed up of his own accord. He had been a sheep rustler just after the war but now, as far as was known, was merely a go-between for usurers. He informed partly by vocation and partly because he deluded himself that by so doing he could carry on his activity with impunity. This activity he considered honest and sensible compared with that of armed robbery, befitting the father of a family, and his past as a sheep-stealer he wrote off as an error of youth. Now, without a lira of capital, simply by handling the money of others, he managed to support a wife and three children and was even able to set some aside to be invested later in a little business: for to stand measuring out cloth behind the counter of a little shop was his life-long dream.

But his easy and lucrative living was connected with his youthful error and the fact that he was an ex-convict: for the gentry who entrusted their money to him, honest men quite above suspicion, supporters of the social order and pillars of the Church, relied on his reputation to prevent their victims lapsing in their payments and to ensure no trouble about secrecy. Indeed, such was the

26

fear that the go-between inspired ('I've left my jacket at the Ucciardone prison,' he used to say as a joke or a threat, meaning that if he killed someone he would go back and fetch it, though as a matter of fact the very thought of prison made him shudder), that debtors paid one hundred per cent interest and dead on time. Rare extensions were granted by applying a cumulative rate of interest, whose net result was that anyone who had obtained a loan, say, to buy the mule necessary to work the few acres of land he owned, found himself after a couple of years minus both mule and land.

Had it not been for his fear, the informer would have reckoned himself happy and an honest man both morally and financially. But terror lurked within him like a rabid dog, growling, panting, slobbering, sometimes suddenly howling in its sleep. For incessant gnawing at the liver and sudden painful stabs at the heart, like a live rabbit's in a dog's mouth, doctors had made diagnosis after diagnosis and prescribed him enough medicines to fill his dressing-table drawer; of his terror the doctors knew nothing.

He was sitting in front of the captain, turned slightly sideways so as not to look him in the face, and nervously twisting his cap, while all the time the dog inside him bit, growled, bit again. The evening was icy cold and the tiny electric stove in the captain's office gave out so little warmth that it made the vast, bare room seem even colder. Even the old-fashioned whitish enamelled tiles with which it was paved looked like ice. Still, the man was sweating; a cold death-shroud enveloped him, chill over the fiery laceration of the *lupara* slugs which were already rending his flesh.

From the moment he had heard of Colasberna's death,

the informer had begun thinking out his story. At each detail he added, each little touch, like a painter standing back from his canvas to judge the effect of a brush-stroke, he would say to himself: 'Perfect. Not another thing needed,' but kept on adding and retouching. And he was still feverishly adding and retouching even as he told it to the captain. But the captain knew, from a voluminous dossier on the police informer, Calogero Dibella, alias *Parrinieddu* or 'Little Priest', that of the two *cosche* or local mafia groups (*cosca*, they had explained to him, meant the thick cluster of artichoke leaves) Dibella was closer to, if not actually a member of, the one which had certain if unprovable connections with public works. As S. was a coastal town, the other *cosca*, younger and more enterprising, mainly concerned itself with the contraband of American cigarettes. He thus foresaw the informer's lie; but in any case it would be useful to watch the man's reactions while telling it.

He listened without interrupting, occasionally adding to Dibella's discomfiture with a distracted nod. In the meanwhile he thought of those other informers buried under a thin layer of soil and dried leaves high in folds of the Apennines. Wretched dregs, soaked in fear and vice; yet they had gambled with death, staking their lives on the razor's edge of a lie between partisans and fascists. The only human emotion they had was the tormenting agony of their own cowardice. From fear of death they faced death every day; until finally it struck, final, permanent, unequivocal death, not the double-cross, the double death of every hour.

The informer of S. was risking his life; sooner or later one *cosca* or the other, either with a double-barrel of *lupara* or a burst from a submachine gun (the two *cosche* also differed in their choice of weapons), would fix him. But between mafia and carabinieri, the two sides between which he played his game of chance, death could come to him only from one side. On this side there was no death; there was only this fair, clean-shaven man in his smart uniform, who lisped, never raised his voice, or treated him with scorn. Yet he was just as much the law as was that gruesome death. To the informer the law was not a rational thing born of reason, but something depending on a man, on the thoughts and the mood of this man here, on the cut he gave himself shaving or a good cup of coffee he has just drunk. To him the law was utterly irrational, created on the spot by those in command, the municipal guard, the sergeant, the chief of police or the magistrate, whoever happened to be administering it. The informer had never, could never have, believed that the law was definitely codified and the same for all; for him between rich and poor, between wise and ignorant, stood the guardians of the law who only used the strong arm on the poor; the rich they protected and defended. It was like a barbed wire entanglement, a wall. The thief who had done time, was involved with the mafia, negotiated extortionate loans and played the informer asked only to find a hole in the wall, a gap in the barbed wire. If he did, he would soon raise enough capital to open his little shop; his elder son he would put into a seminary, either to become a priest or leave before ordination to become, better than a priest, a lawyer. Once over the wall the law would no longer hold terrors. How wonderful it would be to look back on those still behind the wall, behind the barbed wire.

So, tortured by fear, he tried to find some consolation by fondly picturing his future peace, a peace founded on poverty and injustice. But for him the fatal bullet was already cast.

Captain Bellodi, on the contrary, an Emilian from Parma, was by family tradition and personal conviction a republican, a soldier who followed what used to be called 'the career of arms' in a police force, with the dedication of a man who has played his part in a revolution and has seen law created by it. This law, the law of the Republic, which safeguarded liberty and justice, he served and enforced. If he still wore a uniform which he had first put on by chance, if he had not left the service to become a lawyer, the career to which he had been destined, it was because the task of serving and enforcing the law of the Republic was becoming more arduous every day.

The informer would have been astounded to know that the man he was facing, a carabiniere and an officer too, regarded the authority vested in him as a surgeon regards the knife: an instrument to be used with care, precision and certainty; a man convinced that law rests on the idea of justice and that any action taken by the law should be governed by justice. His was a difficult and ungrateful profession; but the informer only saw him as a happy man, happy in the joy of being able to abuse his powers, a joy the more intense the more suffering can be inflicted on others.

Like a shopkeeper displaying his lengths of cheap cotton to country housewives, *Parrinieddu* unwound his roll of lies. His nickname of Little Priest was due to the easy eloquence and hypocrisy he exuded. But, as a result of the officer's silence, his fluency began to leave him,

his words began to sound tearful or strident, and the
pattern he was weaving became incoherent, incredible.

'Don't you think –' the captain quietly asked him after
a while, in a tone of friendly confidence – 'don't you
think it might be more useful to explore other possibili-
ties?' The double-s of the Emilian accent left the word
incomplete and vague and for a moment distracted the
informer from his flow.

Parrinieddu did not reply.

'Don't you think that there's a chance that Colasberna
was done away with for, let us say, a question of interest?
For not having accepted certain proposals? For having
continued, in spite of threats, to land all he could in the
way of contracts?'

Captain Bellodi's predecessors had been in the habit of
questioning the informer in threatening tones with
explicit alternatives of either internment by the police or a
charge of usury. This, instead of frightening *Parrinieddu*,
had given him a certain sense of security. The link was
clear: the police were forcing him to some betrayal and
he just had to produce enough information to keep them
quiet and himself out of trouble. But with someone
treating him kindly and taking him into his confidence,
things were different. So he answered the captain's
question with a disjointed motion of the hands and head:
yes, it was possible.

'And,' continued the captain in the same tone, 'do you
happen to know of anyone who takes an interest in such
matters? I don't mean those who work on contracts; I
mean those who don't, who concern themselves with
helping, with protecting ... It would be enough for me
to know the name of the man who, some months ago,

made certain proposals to Colasberna; proposals, mark you, only proposals ... '

'I know nothing,' said the informer and, encouraged by the captain's gentle manner, his spy's instinct soared like a lark trilling its joy at being able to hurt. 'I know nothing,' he repeated, 'but, taking a shot in the dark, I'd say that the proposals were made either by Ciccio La Rosa or by Saro Pizzuco ... ' But already that giddy flight of joy had turned into a headlong drop, a stone plummeting down into the very centre of his being, his fear.

*   *   *

'Another question in the House,' said His Excellency. ' "Is the Minister aware of the serious acts of violence which have recently taken place in Sicily and what steps does he intend to take ... ?" etc. etc. The communists, as usual. It seems that they are referring to the murder of that contractor ... What was his name?'

'Colasberna, Excellency.'

'Colasberna ... A communist, it seems ... '

'A socialist, Excellency.'

'You will make that distinction. You are stubborn, my friend, allow me to tell you. Communist or socialist, what's the difference?'

'At the present juncture ... '

'For heaven's sake, no explanations. Even I read the papers sometimes, you know ... '

'I would never take the liberty of ... '

'Good. Now, to avoid this ... '

'Colasberna.'

'This Colasberna becoming a martyr in the communist ... sorry, I mean socialist cause, we must find out who killed him. Pretty damn quickly, too, so that the Minister can reply that Colasberna was the victim of a question of interest, or had been after somebody's wife and politics had nothing to do with it.'

'The investigation is going well. It is clearly a mafia crime, but nothing to do with politics. Captain Bellodi ... '

'Who is this Bellodi?'

'He commands the Carabinieri in C. He's been in Sicily some months now ... '

'Right. Now here's the point: I've been wanting to talk to you for some while about Bellodi. This fellow, my dear friend, has a fixation about the mafia. One of those Northerners with a head full of prejudices who begin to see the mafia in everything before they even get off the ferry-boat. If he says that Colasberna was killed by the mafia, we're sunk. I don't know whether you read what a journalist wrote some weeks ago about the kidnapping of that landowner ... What was his name?'

'Mendolia.'

'That's it, Mendolia. He said things to make your hair stand on end. That the mafia exists, that it is a powerful organization, that it controls everything: flocks, fruit and vegetables, public works and Greek vases ... That about Greek vases is priceless ... like a comic postcard. What I say is this: let's have a little sense of responsibility ... Do you believe in the mafia?'

'Well, er ... '

'And you?'

'No, I don't.'

'Good man! We two, both Sicilians, don't believe in

the mafia. That ought to mean something to you, who evidently do. But I can understand you. You aren't Sicilian and prejudices die hard. In time you will be convinced that it is all a build-up. But, meanwhile, now for heaven's sake keep an eye on the investigations of this man Bellodi ... And you, who don't believe in the mafia, try to get something done. Send someone, someone who knows how to handle things. We don't want any trouble with Bellodi, but ... *Ima summis mutare*. Do you understand Latin? Not Horace's: mine, I mean.'

* * *

Paolo Nicolosi, tree-pruner by trade, born at B. on December 14th, 1920, now domiciled and resident in S., at No. 97 Via Cavour, had been missing for five days. On the fourth day his wife had gone back to see the sergeant-major, who, this time, began to take things seriously. His report lay on Captain Bellodi's desk and 'No. 97 Via Cavour' was underlined in red. The captain was pacing up and down the room smoking furiously; he was waiting to hear from the Records Office and from the Magistrature if Paolo Nicolosi had a criminal record or there were any outstanding charges against him.

Colasberna had been shot from the corner of Via Cavour and Piazza Garibaldi. Having fired the shots, the murderer would hardly have come forward into the square where there was a bus with about fifty people on board and a fritter-seller only two paces from the dead man. It was more logical to assume that he had made his get-away down Via Cavour. The time had been six thirty in the morning and the report stated that Nicolosi was to have gone to prune trees at the Fondachello farm, about an hour away on foot. Perhaps, when the killer was running down the street, Nicolosi had come out and recognized him. But how many other people had seen him? The murderer could have counted on Nicolosi's silence, as on that of the fritter-seller and all the others, had he been either a resident or someone well-known in the town; but certainly, in a crime of this sort, he must have been a hired assassin from elsewhere. We learn from America.

No flights of fancy, the major had warned him. All right, then, no flights of fancy. But Sicily is all a realm of fantasy and what can anyone do there without imagination? Nothing but plain facts, then, which were these: a man called Colasberna had been killed just as he was getting on a bus for Palermo in Piazza Garibaldi at six thirty in the morning. The murderer had shot him from the corner of Via Cavour and Piazza Garibaldi and made his escape down Via Cavour. On the same day, at the same time, a man who lived in the same Via Cavour was leaving home, or just about to. According to his wife, she had been expecting him back in the evening, at about Angelus time as usual, she said, but he had never turned up then, nor for the next five days. At the Fondachello farm they say that they've not seen him; they were expecting him that day but he never appeared. He had vanished, together with his mule and his implements, between the door of his house and the Fondachello farm, some four or five miles apart. He had vanished without a trace.

If Nicolosi turned out to have a criminal record or to be involved in some way with the underworld, then he might possibly have gone into hiding; or maybe someone had settled a grudge and covered up all trace of him. But if he hadn't; if there were no reason for him to make any premeditated disappearance; if he were not a man to have any direct or indirect accounts to settle with the underworld; then his disappearance could be definitely, without any flight of fancy, connected with the murder of Colasberna.

The captain did not at that moment take into account a chance of Nicolosi's disappearance being in some way connected with his wife; of it being, in other words, one of those crimes of passion, so useful alike to mafia and police. Ever since the time when, in the sudden silence of the orchestra pit, during *Cavalleria Rusticana*, the cry of '*Hanno ammazzato cumpari Turiddu!*' ('They've killed Turiddu!') first chilled the spines of opera enthusiasts, criminal statistics and number symbols of the lottery in Sicily have had closer links between cuckoldom and violent death. A crime of passion is solved at once: so it is an asset to the police; it is also punished lightly: so it is an asset to the mafia. Nature imitates art; Turiddu Macca, having been killed on the stage by Mascagni's music and Compare Alfio's knife, began to figure on tourist maps – and autopsy tables – of Sicily. Sometimes, though, either by knife or by *lupara* (luckily no longer by music) the Alfios get the worst of it. At that moment Captain Bellodi did not take this into account; a distraction that was to bring him a minor reprimand.

Negative reports on Paolo Nicolosi were brought back by Sergeants D'Antona and Pitrone from the Magistrature and the Records Office – no charges outstanding, no previous convictions. The captain was satisfied, but impatient; impatient to hurry over to S. and talk with Nicolosi's wife, with some of the missing man's friends, with the sergeant-major; to question the people at Fondachello and then, should circumstances warrant, have a word with the two men named by the informer, La Rosa and Pizzuco.

It was already midday. He ordered his car and hurried downstairs, feeling like singing from mounting excitement, and actually humming as he made his way to the canteen. There he ate a couple of sandwiches and drank a hot coffee, a coffee made specially for him by the carabiniere-barman, with the right amount of coffee and all the skill of a Neapolitan trying to get on the right side of his superior.

The day was cold and bright, the country limpid: trees, fields and rocks gave an impression of gelid fragility as though a gust of wind or an impact would shatter them with a tinkle of breaking glass. The air, too, vibrated like glass to the engine of the little Fiat 600. Overhead large black crows flew around as if in a glass maze, suddenly wheeling, dropping or circling up vertically as though between invisible walls. The road was deserted. In the back seat Sergeant D'Antona held out of the window the muzzle of his sten-gun, his finger on the trigger. Only a month before on this road the bus from S. to C. had been held up and all the passengers robbed. The bandits, all minors, were already in San Francesco Prison.

The sergeant, watching the road uneasily, thought of his income and his expenses, of pay and wife, pay and television set, pay and sick children. The carabiniere-driver thought about a film, *Europe by Night*, which he had seen the evening before, and of his surprise at Cocinelle being a man, a man indeed! Behind this thought, which was more vision than thought, lay a worry, deep down and hidden lest the captain guess it, at not having eaten in barracks and if they would be in time to get anything with the Carabinieri of S. But that captain – what a man! – did guess and told the two of them, sergeant and driver, that they would have to scrounge something for themselves at S. and that he was sorry for not having thought of it before leaving. The driver blushed and thought, not for the first time: 'He's a kind man, but he reads my mind.' The sergeant said that he was not hungry and could go without eating till next day.

At S. the sergeant-major, who had not been warned, came out with his mouth full, his face red with surprise and mortification. He'd had to leave a plate of roast mutton; cold, it would be disgusting; heated up, worse; mutton must be eaten hot, swimming in fat and savoury with pepper. Oh, well, it's a penance; let's hear the news.

News there was. The sergeant-major nodded his approval; though, to tell the truth, not altogether convinced of a link between the shooting of Colasberna and Nicolosi's disappearance. He sent for the widow, a couple of Nicolosi's friends and the man's brother-in-law. 'Widow' was the word he used as he sent the carabiniere to fetch her, for he had no doubt the man was dead. A quiet-living man like Nicolosi only vanishes for so long for that one simple reason. Meanwhile, he invited the captain for a bite; the captain declined, saying that he had already eaten.

'So you've eaten, have you!' thought the sergeant-major, his resentment chill as the fat on his mutton chops by now.

She was pretty, the widow; with dark brown hair and jet black eyes, fine features, and a serene expression, but a vaguely mischievous smile on her lips. She was not shy. Her dialect was comprehensible so the captain did not need the sergeant-major to act as interpreter; he himself asked the woman the meaning of certain words and sometimes she found the right Italian equivalent or explained by a phrase in dialect. The captain had known many Sicilians, during his partisan period and, later, among the carabinieri. He had also read Giovanni Meli with Francesco Lanza's notes and Ignazio Buttitta with the facing translation by Quasimodo.

That day her husband had been up just before six. She had heard him get up, in the dark, not wanting to wake her. He had been a very considerate man – 'had been', just like that – for evidently she shared the sergeant-major's opinion. But she woke up as she did every morning; and, as usual, told him that the coffee was ready in the sideboard – all it needed was heating up; then she had got back to sleep; not quite asleep, though, but dozing. She heard her husband moving about in the kitchen, then go downstairs to open the street door of the stable. In five or ten minutes, by the time he had got the mule ready, she had again dropped off to sleep. A clink of metal woke her; it was her husband, come up again to fetch his cigarettes and, fumbling on the bedside table in the dark, had knocked over a little silver Sacred Heart, given to her by an aunt who was Mother Superior at the Immacolata Convent. Almost wide awake, she asked her husband what was the matter. 'Nothing,' was his reply, 'go to sleep. I've forgotten my cigarettes.' 'Put the light on,' she said, wide awake now. He said there was no need, then asked her whether she had been woken by two shots fired near by, or by him knocking over the Sacred Heart. That was just like him, she said, capable of blaming himself all day for having woken her. He really had loved her.

'And did you hear the two shots?'

'No. In my sleep I hear every sound in the house, my husband's movements, but outside there might be the fireworks for Santa Rosalia and I'd not wake.'

'What happened next?'

'I put on the light, the little light beside me, sat up in bed and asked him what had happened, what the two shots had been. My husband said: "I don't know, but running down the street I saw ... "'

'Who?' The captain rapped in sudden excitement, leaning across the desk towards the woman. Sudden alarm distorted her features; for a moment she looked ugly. The captain leaned back again in his chair and, in a quiet voice, again asked: 'Who?'

'He said a name I don't remember, or perhaps a nick-name. Now I come to think of it, it might have been a nickname.'

She used the word *ingiuria* and for the first time the captain needed the sergeant-major's talents as inter-preter.

'Nickname,' said the sergeant-major, 'almost every-body here has one, some so offensive that they really are "injuries".'

'It might have been an *ingiuria*,' said the captain, 'but it might also have been some odd surname sounding like an *ingiuria*. Had you ever heard your husband use the name or *ingiuria* before ... ? Try to remember. It's very important.'

'I'm not sure I'd ever heard it before.'

'Try to remember ... and in the meanwhile tell me what else he said or did.'

'He said nothing else. He just left.'

For some minutes, ever since the woman had shown sudden alarm, the sergeant-major's face had been frozen into an expression of baleful incredulity. That, according to him, had been the moment to put on the screw, to frighten her enough to force it out of her, that name or nickname. Sure as God, she had it stamped on her memory. The captain, on the other hand, was being kinder than ever.

'Who does he think he is? Arsène Lupin?' thought the sergeant-major, whose reading days were so far behind him that he mistook burglar for policeman.

'Try to remember that *ingiuria*,' said the captain, 'and in the meanwhile the sergeant-major will be kind enough to offer us some coffee.'

'Coffee too,' thought the sergeant-major. 'It's bad enough not to give her a proper go over, but coffee ... !'

'Yes, sir,' was all he said.

The captain began to talk about Sicily, at its loveliest when most rugged and barren; and how intelligent the Sicilians were. An archaeologist had told him how swift and deft the peasants were during excavations, much more than specialized workmen from the North. It's not true, he said, that Sicilians are lazy or lack initiative.

The coffee came and he was still talking about Sicily and Sicilians. The woman drank hers with little sips,

41

showing some refinement for a pruner's wife. The captain was now passing Sicilian literature in review from Verga to *The Leopard*, dwelling on a particular aspect of literature, *ingiurie*; how they often gave an accurate picture of a whole character in a single word. The woman understood little of this, nor did the sergeant-major; but some things not understood by the mind are understood by the heart; and in their Sicilian hearts the captain's words rustled like music.

'How well he talks,' thought the woman and the sergeant-major. 'Yes, he can talk all right. Better than Terracini,'* whom, apart from his ideas of course, he considered the greatest orator he had ever heard at any of the political meetings which he had to attend as a matter of duty.

'There are *ingiurie* which reveal a person's physical characteristic features or defects,' said the captain, 'and others which reflect his moral character. Still others refer to a particular happening or episode. Then there are hereditary *ingiurie* which include a whole family and can also be found on the maps of the register of landed property ... But let us proceed in order. Of the *ingiurie* which deal with characteristic features or defects, the most banal are: "one-eye", "limper", "lop-sided", "left-handed" ... Was the *ingiuria* your husband said like any of those?'

'No,' said the woman, shaking her head.

'Then there's likenesses – to animals, trees, objects ... For example, "cat" for a man who has grey eyes, or something that makes him look like a cat. I knew a man nicknamed *Lu chiuppu*, "poplar", owing to his height

*A prominent communist senator.

42

and a sort of quiver he had – that was how I had it explained. Objects ... let's see, nicknames due to a likeness to something ... '

'I know a man nicknamed "bottle",' said the sergeant-major, 'and he really is the shape of a bottle.'

"If I may,' said Carabiniere Sposito, who had sat so still he had become almost invisible in the room, 'if I may, I can tell you a few *ingiurie* which are names of objects. "Lantern", for one whose eyes pop out like lanterns; "stewed pear", for one rotten with disease; *vircuocu* – "apricot" – I don't know why, perhaps for a blank look; "Divine Host" for someone with a white round face like a Host ... '

The sergeant-major gave a meaning cough; he did not allow jokes about persons or things in any way connected with religion. Sposito stopped.

The captain looked inquiringly at the woman. She shook her head once or twice. The sergeant-major made a sudden violent movement, his eyes like watery slits between their lids, leaning forward to look at her. Suddenly, as if the word had been brought up by a sudden hiccup, she said: '*Zicchinetta.*'

'*Zecchinetta*,' promptly translated Sposito, 'a game of chance: it's played with Sicilian cards ... '

The sergeant-major gave him a glare; now they had the name, the time for philology was past; whether the word meant a game of cards or a saint in paradise was unimportant (and his instinct for the chase roused the sound of hunting horns in his head, making the saint in paradise bump a nose against Sicilian cards).

The captain, on the contrary, had felt a sudden, sombre sense of discouragement; of disillusion, helpless-

43

ness. That name or *ingiuria* or whatever it was, was finally out; but it had only come out at the second when the sergeant-major had suddenly seemed to become for her a terrifying threat of inquisition, of condemnation. Maybe she had remembered the name from the very moment her husband had uttered it and not forgotten it at all. Or else her sudden desperate fear had brought it back. Anyway, without the sergeant-major, without that ominous transformation of his from a fat, jovial man to the incarnation of menace, they might never have got the name out of her.

'Give me time for a shave,' said the sergeant-major, 'and I'll soon find out whether this *Zicchinetta* is a local or not. My barber knows everyone.'

'All right,' said the captain wearily; and the sergeant-major asked himself: 'What's up with the man?' Disillusionment, with the captain, had brought on a stab of homesickness; the ray of sun which slanted down on to the table through golden specks of dust, shone for him on throngs of girls on bicycles on the roads of Emilia, on a filigree of trees against a white sky, and on a big house where town gave way to country, a house mellow in evening light and in his memory. He repeated to himself the words of a poet from those parts – 'where thou art missing from our hallowed evening custom' – words written by a poet for a dead brother. In self-pity for his exile, in his disillusionment, Captain Bellodi felt a faint premonition of death.

The woman gave him an apprehensive look, the ray of sunshine falling on the table between them, separating them in a remoteness which, for him, had a sense of unreality and, for her, an obsessive nightmare quality.

44

'What sort of a man was your husband?' asked the captain; and as he put the question he found it natural to use the past tense.

The woman, in her daze, did not understand.

'I would like to know about his character, his habits, his friends.'

'He was a good man: work, home, was his life. On days he wasn't working he'd spend an hour or two at the smallholders' club. On Sundays he'd take me to the cinema. He had few friends, all very respectable, the mayor's brother, a municipal guard ... '

'Had he ever any quarrels, rows about interest, enemies?'

'Never. Everyone liked him. He wasn't a local and strangers are all right here.'

'Oh, of course, he wasn't a local! How did you meet him, then?'

'At a wedding. A relation of mine married a girl from his village, and I went to the wedding with my brother. He saw me there; and, when my relation came back from his honeymoon, he asked him to apply to my father to marry me. My father made inquiries, then spoke to me. He said: "He's a decent young fellow, with a very good job." "I don't even know what he looks like," I said. "I wanted to meet him first." He came one Sunday, not as engaged, but as a friend; he hardly opened his mouth, just looked at me all the time as if bewitched. Spellbound, my relation said; as if I'd put a spell on him. He was only joking, of course. I decided to marry him.'

'And did you love him?'

'Of course; we were married.'

The sergeant-major came back, reeking of barber's

cheap eau-de-Cologne. 'Nothing,' he said, then moved behind the woman's back and mimicked frantically towards the captain to get rid of her, that there was red-hot news, amazing news about the woman. '*Zicchinetta* be damned,' his head-high, rotating hand seemed to say.

The woman was shown out. Breathlessly the sergeant-major poured out the news that she had a lover, a man called Passerello, a dues-collector from the electric light company. Reliable information, from Don Ciccio the barber.

The captain showed no surprise. Instead, he asked about *Zicchinetta*, thus reversing the good old custom of giving priority to the passionate elements of a crime, if they exist.

'Don Ciccio,' said the sergeant-major, 'states categorically that there is no one in the town with that name or *ingiuria*; and in such matters Don Ciccio is infallible ... If he says poor Nicolosi was a cuckold, then the fact's signed and sealed. So let's get hold of this Passerello and put the squeeze on him ... '

'No,' said the captain, 'we'll take a little trip instead, and pay a visit to your colleague at B.'

'I get it,' said the sergeant-major, rather put out.

They drove along the coast to B. in silence, the calm sea reflecting the muted tones of the sky. They found the sergeant-major in his office; conspicuous on his desk was a dossier concerning one Diego Marchica, known as *Zicchinetta*, released from prison only a month or so before thanks to an amnesty. The dossier was in such a conspicuous position because of some new information about gambling, and *zecchinetta* in particular, a game that Marchica was wont to play at the sportsman's club, losing largish sums and settling them on the spot, almost impossible for an unemployed farmhand to do unless he had secret – and certainly illicit – sources of income.

Born in 1917, Marchica had begun his career in 1935: housebreaking; convicted 1938; arson. Those whose evidence had convicted him for theft had had their sheaves of grain burned on the threshing-floor: acquitted for lack of evidence. August 1943: armed robbery; retention of military weapons; criminal association. Tried by the Americans: acquitted (with what justification was not clear). 1946: membership of an armed band; captured during a shooting incident with the carabinieri: convicted. 1951: murder; insufficient evidence; acquitted. 1955: attempted murder during a brawl; convicted. The 1951 murder charge was interesting. It was a murder committed on behalf of a third party, according to the confessions of his accomplices to the carabinieri, confessions which of course melted like snow during the preliminary proceedings. The two men who had confessed displayed bruises, abrasions and excoriations to doctors and judge, all due, of course, to torture by the carabinieri. It was odd that Marchica, the only one not to talk, should have no single bruise to show to the judge. A sergeant and two carabinieri were put on trial for obtaining confessions extorted by violence, and found innocent. This meant that the confessions should have been considered spontaneous. But the case was never reopened, or maybe the file was on its rounds in the labyrinth of the law.

The notes described Marchica as a very shrewd and

cunning criminal, a reliable hired assassin, but capable, when gambling or in his cups, of sudden outbursts of rage, as indicated by the charge of attempted murder during a brawl. In the file there was also a report on a political meeting held by the Honourable Member Livigni. This gentleman, encircled by the flower of the local mafia, on his right the local grey eminence, Don Calogero Guicciardo, and on his left Marchica, had appeared on the centre balcony of the Alvarez palazzo. At a certain point in his speech he had said, verbatim: 'I am accused of being associated with members of the mafia and so with the mafia itself. But I assure you that I have never yet been able to find out what the mafia is or even if it exists. I give you my word with the clear conscience of a good Catholic and a citizen, that I have never met one member of the mafia.' Whereupon, from the direction of Via La Lumia, at the end of the piazza where the communists usually congregated during an opposition meeting, a loud voice demanded: 'And those characters up there with you, what are they? Seminarists?' A wave of laughter swept through the crowd, while the Honourable Member, ignoring the question, plunged into a peroration about his programme for agricultural reform.

This report was included in Marchica's dossier as a warning of the protection which he might have in the event of his arrest. The sergeant-major of B. knew his job.

*   *   *

'There's something afoot,' said the old man, 'something I don't like. The police are up to something.'

'They're shadow-boxing,' said the young man.

'Don't get the idea all police are stupid. Some could take the shoes off the likes of you and you'd be walking barefoot before you realized ... In '35, I remember, there was a sergeant here with the nose of a bloodhound, he even looked like one. When something happened, off he'd go on the trail and get you like a newly-weaned hare. What a nose he had, that son of a ... ! He was born a policeman, as one is born a priest or a cuckold. Don't you believe that a man wears horns because a woman puts them there or becomes a priest because, at a certain moment, he gets a vocation; they're born to it. And a man doesn't become a policeman because he needs a job or reads a recruiting poster; he becomes one because he was born one. Mark you, I'm only talking about real police; some, poor things, are as good as gold; but I don't call them police. A decent man like that sergeant-major who was here during the war – what was his name? – the one who got on so well with the Americans, nobody could call him a policeman. He'd do us favours; and we'd return them, with cases of pasta and demijohns of oil. A gentleman. Not a born policeman, but not stupid either ... We are inclined to call policemen all those with that flame emblem and V.E. on their caps ... '

'They've no V.E. any more ... '

'Nor they do; I always forget we've no king now ... But among them there are stupid ones, good ones and then real police, born so. It's the same with priests. Could you call Padre Frazzo a priest? The best one can say of him is that he's a good father to his children. But, take Padre Spina, there's a born priest for you.'

'And what about the cuckolds?'

'I'm just coming to them. Suppose a man finds his wife has been betraying him and makes a shambles; he's no born cuckold. But if he pretends not to notice or resigns himself, then he is ... Now I'll tell you what a born policeman is like. He arrives in town; you begin to make up to him, do him favours, ingratiate yourself. If he's married, you even take your wife to call; your wives become friends, you become friends; people see you and think you are all friends together. You kid yourself that he thinks you're a nice person, considerate, a loyal friend; but for him, you're always what his office files say you are. If you've ever been fined, then in his eyes, all the time, even when he's drinking coffee in your parlour, you're a man who's been fined. If you happen to break the law, a trifle, even if only you and he know and not even God Almighty has seen you, he'll fine you just like that. So if it's anything more serious ... In '27, I remember, there was a sergeant-major of carabiniere who practically lived in my house. Not a day passed without his wife and children paying us a visit. We were such friends that his youngest son, a kid of three, used to call my wife "aunt". One day he turned up in my house with a warrant for my arrest. It was his duty, I know; they were difficult times – there was Mori – but the way he treated me ... just as if we'd never met, never known one another ... And the way he treated my wife when she went to the barracks for news. He was like a rabid dog. Whoever takes up with a copper can say goodbye to his wine and cigars, so they say. With that sergeant-major I certainly said goodbye to a good deal of mine, the amount he drank and smoked.'

'In '27,' said the young man, 'during fascism, things

were different. Mussolini named members of Parliament and mayors. Did just what he liked. Nowadays it's the people who elect.'

'The people,' said the old man, sneering, 'the people were cuckolds then and they still are. The only difference is that fascism hung only one flag on the people's horns and democracy lets everyone hang one on his own horns and choose his own colour. We're back to the old argument. Not only men, but entire nations are born cuckolds, cuckolds from olden times, generation after generation ... '

'I don't consider myself a cuckold,' said the young man.

'Nor do I. But we, my dear boy, walk on the horns of others; like dancers ... ' and the old man got up and did a few tripping dance steps, mimicking the balance and rhythm of one hopping from the tip of one horn to another.

The young man laughed; it was a pleasure to hear the other talk. The cold astute violence for which he had been famous in his youth, the calculated risk, the presence of mind, the swiftness of hand, all the qualities, in short, which had caused him to be regarded with such respect and dread, sometimes seemed to ebb from him like the sea from the shore, leaving empty shells of wisdom on the sands of the years. 'He becomes a real philosopher at times,' thought the young man, mistaking philosophy for a sort of play of mirrors in which a long memory and a brief future reflect twilit thoughts and vague distorted images of reality. At other times the older man would reveal how hard and merciless he had been; and it was strange that when he was delivering his severest and most realistic judgments on the world, his speech was literally strewn with the words 'horns' and 'cuckold', often with different meanings and nuances, but always to express scorn.

'The people, democracy,' said the old man, sitting down again, slightly out of breath after his demonstration of how to walk on people's horns, 'are fine inventions; things dreamed up at a desk by people who know how to shove one word up the backside of another, and strings of words up the backside of humanity, with all due respect ... With all due respect to humanity, I mean. Humanity's a forest of horns, thicker than the woods of Ficuzza when they really were woods. And d'you know who the people are who have fun walking on its horns? Firstly – bear this well in mind – priests. Secondly: politicians; and the more they say they're with the people, out for the people's welfare, the more they trample on their horns. Thirdly: people like you and me ... It's true that there is the risk of putting a foot wrong and being gored, for me as for priests and politicians; but even if a horn rips into my guts, it's still a horn; and anybody who wears one on his head is a cuckold. The satisfaction of it, by God, the satisfaction! I'm done, a goner, but you, you're nothing but cuckolds ... !

'By the way, speaking of cuckolds, I wonder about that *Parrinieddu* ... with all this coming and going of police .. he has a hand in it I suspect ... he must have. Yesterday, when I ran into him, his face changed colour; he pretended not to see me and vanished up an alley. I say to myself: "I've let you play the spy because you've a living to earn, I know; but you must do it with discretion, not set yourself against Mother Church" '; and

52

by Mother Church he meant his own inviolable self and the sacred knot of friendships which he represented and protected.

Continuing to address himself to *Parrinieddu* as though the man were present, he said with icy solemnity: 'And if you set yourself against Mother Church, my friend, what can I do about it? Nothing. I can only tell you that in your friends' hearts you're a dead man.'

They were silent a while, as though reciting a requiem for the man who was dead in their hearts. Then the old man said: 'Diego ought to go away for a little holiday, I think. I seem to remember he has a sister in Genoa ... '

* * *

Diego Marchica was arrested at 9.30 in the evening at the sportsman's club. The sergeant-major of B. had intended to kill two birds with one stone but caught only one. He had hoped to catch gamblers red-handed playing *zecchinetta* and to run Diego in, but all the players, including Diego, had been engaged in an innocent game of *briscola*; evidently a lookout had tipped them off about the arrival of the carabinieri. However, *briscola* or no, Diego, at first indignant, then submissive, was hauled off to the barracks amid the comments of by-standers. Those which reached the ears of Diego and the carabinieri were of surprise and commiseration ('What's he done? Just minding his own business, wasn't he? Not interfering with anyone, was he?'); but, *sotto voce*, almost inaudibly, they expressed almost unanimous hopes that Diego would spend the rest of his life behind the bars he was so used to.

53

While Diego was being arrested at B., at S. *Parrinieddu* became the number which, in the art of foretelling lottery numbers, is assigned to the victim of a violent death; the only form, apart from his immortal soul, in which he was to survive.

The last twenty-four hours of the life of Calogero Dibella, known as *Parrinieddu*, were spent in a kind of dream, of crossing a boundless forest, thick as a bramble-bush and so lofty and dense that it shuts out the light. For the first time in his career as an informer he had given the carabinieri a thread to pull which, if they went about it the right way, could unravel a tissue of friendships and interests interwoven with his own existence. Usually his information only concerned people outside these friendships and interests; youths who saw a hold-up at the cinema one night and went out next day and held up a bus; small-time crooks, in fact, isolated and without protection. But this time things were different. It was true that he had given two names, of which one, La Rosa's, had nothing to do with the case; the other, though, was the right thread, a certainty. And ever since he had mentioned that name he had known no peace; his body was a terror-soaked sponge, absorbing even a gnawing liver and agonizing stabs at the heart.

Pizzuco, who had invited him to a bitter vermouth at the Café Gulino, as so often in the past, was astounded at *Parrinieddu*'s refusal and abrupt flight; though not particularly bright, he wondered about it for the rest of the day. *Parrinieddu*, for his part, was so rattled that he spent the day attributing sinister meanings to that offer of a bitter vermouth, bitter betrayal, bitter death, over-looking the well-known fact that Pizzuco suffered from what the doctors called cirrhosis due to his fondness for Averna's bitter vermouth – a beverage which made him proclaim his faith as Separatist and ex-soldier of the Volunteer Army for Sicilian Independence; though according to police records he had merely been a minor accomplice of the bandit Giuliano.

Many others noticed *Parrinieddu*'s peculiar behaviour, his apprehensive walk like someone with a mastiff at his heels; those who feared him and wished to avoid him noticed it most. Then had come that meeting with the man he feared most, a man capable of knowing – or guessing – what had been said in confidence between office walls. He had pretended not to see him, turned a corner at once; but the other had seen him, and followed him with his impassive gaze from beneath heavily-lidded eyes.

Since that meeting, the informer's last twenty-four hours had been all anguished frenzy. Longing for flight, which he knew to be impossible, alternated with visions of himself as a corpse. Flight was in the prolonged whistle of a train, in the countryside unfolding from the train window, towns rolling slowly by full of bright flowers and women at windows; then, suddenly, along came a tunnel, the word death hammered by the rhythm of the train, and death's black waters closing over him.

Without realizing it, by three days of anxiety, of false steps, of visible apprehension and nervousness, he had dug his own grave. Now he thought he'd be shot down, 'like a dog'; but he thought death was coming to him because of his betrayal, that it was known or suspected, and not because his terror had turned to madness and he had become the living image of treachery. The two names he had let slip were only in the memory of Captain Bellodi who, not wishing to have another corpse on his hands, had every intention of protecting the informer; but *Parrinieddu*, his nerves ragged from anxiety, saw his information floating round like chaff. Beyond hope, at dawn of what was to be his last day, he wrote the captain two names on a flimsy sheet of airmail paper, and the words: 'I'm dead', then, as if finishing off a letter, ended 'With regards, Calogero Dibella'. He posted the letter while the town was still deserted; all that day he spent either wandering about the streets, or rushing home a dozen times, determined to shut himself up there, then coming out as many times to get himself killed once and for all; just when he had finally made up his mind to hide, two unerring pistol shots got him on his own doorstep.

The captain read the letter only after hearing of the death. After giving instructions to the sergeant-major of B. to arrest Marchica, Captain Bellodi, tired out, returned to C. and went straight to his quarters. When told of Dibella's death, he went down to the office; and there was the letter in the afternoon's post. It gave him a great shock.

The man had left this life with one final denunciation, the most accurate and explosive one he had ever made. The two names were in the middle of the page and, beneath, almost at the foot, that desperate message, the 'regards' and the signature. It was not the importance of the denunciation which made such an impression on the captain, but the agony, the despair which had provoked it. Those 'regards' made him feel brotherly compassion and anguished distress, the compassion and distress of one who under appearances classified, defined and rejected, suddenly discovers the naked tragic human heart. By his death, by his last farewell, the informer had come into a closer, more human relationship; this might be unpleasant, vexatious; but in the feelings and thoughts of the man who shared them they brought a response of sympathy, of spiritual sympathy.

Suddenly this state of mind gave way to rage. The captain felt a wave of resentment at the narrow limits in which the law compelled him to act; like his subordinates he found himself longing for exceptional powers, exceptional liberty of action; a longing he had always condemned in them. A few months' suspension in Sicily of constitutional guarantees, and the evil could be uprooted for ever. Then he remembered Mori's repression of the mafia under fascism and rejected this alternative. But his anger smouldered on, his Northerner's anger against the whole of Sicily, the only region in the whole of Italy actually to have been given liberty during the fascist dictatorship, the liberty of safety of life and property. How many other liberties this liberty of theirs had cost, the Sicilians did not know or want to know. In the dock at the assizes they had seen all the *Dons* and *zii*, the election riggers and even those Commanders of the Order of the Crown of Italy, the doctors and lawyers who intrigued with or protected the underworld. Weak or corrupt magistrates had been dismissed; complaisant officials removed. For peasant, smallholder, shepherd and sulphur-miner, dictatorship had spoken this language of freedom.

'And perhaps that's why there are so many fascists in Sicily,' thought the captain. 'They never saw fascism as

57

buffoonery or, like us, lived out its full tragic consequences after September 8th; but it's not only that. It's because in the condition they were in, one liberty was enough, they would not have known what to do with any others.' But this was not an objective opinion.

As he pursued these thoughts, at times clear and at others confused, for he lacked knowledge, he was already on his way through the night to S., a night which the cold white headlights made even vaster and more mysterious, an endless vault of splendid crystals and of glittering apparitions.

The sergeant-major of S. had had a terrible day, and was about to wade through an even worse night, with silent insidious waters of sleep waiting to drown him at any moment. From the neighbouring town he had brought in Marchica who, to tell the truth, had caused no trouble and, indeed, seemed half asleep like a puppy at its mother's dugs: he had gone peacefully into the guard-room and, even before the door was closed behind him, thrown himself, like a sack of bones, on the plank bed.

And, as if Marchica were not enough, the last straw for the sergeant-major had been another corpse. It was enough to drive the most placid of men crazy; but the sergeant-major, with his pangs of hunger and his weariness, just felt sleepy. Then just as he was slipping off for a cup of coffee he was stopped on the very threshold of the bar by the voice of the captain, who had arrived that minute, which showed what an unlucky star he had, at least in his relations with his superiors. Instead, the captain joined him in a coffee, and insisted on paying for both, in spite of the barman saying what a pleasure it was for the bar to offer a coffee impersonally to the *Signor Capitano* and the *Signor Maresciallo*, thus making the sergeant-major's ill humour foam silently like a glass of beer. 'Now he'll think I come in here and drink free,' he was thinking. But the captain had quite other worries.

The body of *Parrinieddu*, covered by a bluish cloth, still lay on the pavement. The carabiniere picket raised the cloth; the body was contracted in the dark womb of death as though in prenatal sleep. 'I'm dead,' he had written, and here he was dead by his own doorstep. Through the closed windows came the moans of his wife, and the murmur of neighbours hurried in to comfort her. The captain looked at the body for a moment, then made a sign for it to be covered again. The sight of the dead always disturbed him, particularly this one. Followed by the sergeant-major, he went back to barracks.

His plan was this: to arrest forthwith the two mentioned in *Parrinieddu*'s farewell message and interrogate, separately and almost simultaneously, under conditions and in a way which he had already carefully worked out, both of them and the third man already under arrest. The sergeant-major considered the arrest of Rosario Pizzuco an easy matter, that is to say, without troublesome consequences. But, with the second name, the one that the informer had only had the courage to write when dead, he had visions of successive calamities rolling down from one step to another like a rubber ball, till finally they bounced up into the face of Sergeant-Major Arturo Ferlisi, commanding the Carabiniere Station of S.; not for much longer, the way things were going. In his bewilderment he took upon himself to point out respectfully the consequences to the captain. The captain had already weighed them up. There was nothing for it, then, but to tie up the donkey where its owner wanted it; Sergeant-Major Ferlisi felt he was tying it up amid a lot of crockery and that the effect of its kick would be something to remember for the rest of his days.

*   *   *

'I just can't understand, it's unthinkable; a man like Don Mariano Arena, upright, devoted to family and parish, old too, and with so many infirmities and crosses to bear ... And they arrest him like a common criminal while, if you'll forgive my saying so, there are so many real ones walking around under our very noses, or rather yours. But I do know how much you personally try to do and I appreciate your work highly, even though it's not for me to give it its full due.'

'Thank you, but we all do our best.'

'No, let me have my say ... When in the middle of the night they knock up an honoured household, yes, honoured, and pull out of bed a poor creature who's also aged and decrepit, and drag him off to jail like a common criminal, causing anguish and consternation to an entire family; no, no, it's not only inhuman, it's rank injustice ... '

'But there are well-founded suspicions that ... '

'Founded? Where and how? Say someone goes out of his mind and sends you a note with my name on it; then you come along here, at dead of night, and, old as I am, without regard for my past record as a citizen, drag me off to jail as if I were anyone ... '

60

'Well, to tell the truth, there *are* some stains on Arena's record ... '

'Stains? Listen to me, my friend, let me talk as a Sicilian and as a man in my position, if that offers any guarantee. The famous Mori wasted blood and tears in these parts ... That was one of the sides of fascism on which it's better not to dwell; and, mark you, I'm no detractor of fascism; some newspapers, in fact, even go as far as to call me one myself ... And was there no good in fascism? Indeed there was, and how ... Now this rabble who call liberty the mud they sling about to besmirch the finest people and the purest sentiments ... But don't let's go into that ... Mori, as I was saying, was a scourge of God here; he swept up all and sundry, guilty and innocent, honest and dishonest, according to his own whims and his spies ... It was a catastrophe for the whole of Sicily, my friend ... And now you come and talk to me of stains. What stains? If you knew Don Mariano Arena as I do, you'd not talk of stains. He's a man, let me tell you, of whom there are few of his kind about. I'm not referring to the integrity of his faith, which to you, rightly or wrongly, may be a matter of indifference; but to his honesty, his love for others, his wisdom ... An exceptional man, I assure you. All the more so when one considers that he is uneducated, uncultured ... but you know how more important a pure heart is than any culture ... Now the arrest of a man like that as a common criminal, and I'm speaking with all sincerity, takes me right back to Mori's times ... '

'But public opinion says that he is a head of the mafia ... '

'Public opinion! What is this public opinion? Rumours in the air, rumours which spread calumny, defamation, cheap vengeance. Anyway, what *is* the mafia? Just another rumour. Everyone says it exists, but where no one knows ... Rumours, will-o'-the-wisp rumours echoing in empty heads, believe me. D'you know what Vittorio Emanuele Orlando used to say? I'll quote you his very words and, far in time as we are from his ideas, when repeated by us they take on even more authority. He used to say – '

'But, from what I have been able to gather from certain phenomena, the mafia *does* exist.'

'You grieve me, my boy, you grieve me. Both as a Sicilian and as the reasonable man I claim to be ... What I unworthily represent, of course, has nothing to do with it ... But both the Sicilian I am and the reasonable man I claim to be rebel against this injustice to Sicily, this insult to reason ... And mind you, I have always spelt the word reason with a small "r" ... Is it really possible to conceive of the existence of a criminal association so vast, so well-organized, so secret and so powerful that it can dominate not only half Sicily, but the entire United States of America? With a head here in Sicily interviewed by reporters and then, poor fellow, vilified by the press in the blackest terms? ... D'you know him? I do. A good man, an exemplary father, an untiring worker. He's got rich, certainly he has, but by his own efforts. And he, too, had his troubles with Mori ... Certain men inspire respect: for their qualities, their savoir-faire, their frankness, their flair for cordial relations, for friendship. Then what you call public opinion, the wind of calumny, gets up at once and says: "These are the heads of the mafia." Now here's something you don't know: these men, the men whom public opinion calls the heads of the mafia, have one quality in common, a quality I would like to find in every man, one which is enough to redeem anyone in the eyes of God – a sense of justice ... naturally, instinctively ... And it's this sense of justice which makes them inspire respect ... '

'That's just the point. The administration of justice is the prerogative of the State; one cannot allow ... '

'I am speaking of the sense of justice, not the administration of justice ... Anyway, suppose we two were squabbling about a piece of land, a will, or a debt; and along comes a third party and settles things between us; then in a sense that third party is administering justice. But you know what might have happened if we had continued litigation before *your* justice, don't you? Years would have passed and finally maybe, from impatience or anger, one or both of us might have resorted to violence ... In short, I don't consider that a man of peace, a peacemaker, is usurping the administration of justice which, of course, is the legitimate prerogative of the State ... '

'Well, if you put things in those terms ... '

'What other terms can I put them in? In the terms of that colleague of yours who wrote a book on the mafia, which if you'll allow me to say so, was so fantastic that I'd never have expected such nonsense from a responsible person ... '

'I found the book very instructive.'

'If you mean you learned something new, all right; but whether the things described in the book really exist is another matter ... Now let's look at it from another point of view. Has there ever been a trial during which it has emerged that there is a criminal association called the mafia and that this association has been definitely responsible for or actually committed a crime? Has any document or witness any proof at all which has ever come to light establishing a sure connection between a crime and the so-called mafia? In the absence of such proof, and if we admit that the mafia exists, I'd say it was a secret association for mutual aid, no more and no less than freemasonry. Why don't you put down some crimes to the freemasons? There's the same amount of proof that the freemasons go in for criminal activity as there is that the mafia does.'

'I believe ... '

'You just believe me. Take my word for it and, in the position I unworthily hold, God knows if I could deceive you, even if I would ... What I say is this: when you, with the authority vested in you, direct – how shall I put it? – your attention to persons indicated by public opinion as belonging to the mafia merely on the grounds of suspicion, with no concrete evidence that the mafia exists or that any single individual belongs to it, then, in the eyes of God, you are committing unjust persecution. This brings us to the case of Don Mariano Arena ... And, incidentally, of this officer of carabinieri who arrested him without thinking twice, with an irresponsibility unworthy, if I may say so, of the uniform he wears. Let us say with Suetonius: *"ne principum quidem virorum insectatione abstinuit ... "* In plain language, this means Don Mariano is revered and respected by the whole town, is a bosom friend of mine and – believe me, I know how to choose my friends – he's also highly thought of by the Honourable Member Livigni and by the Minister Mancuso.'

* * *

The twenty-four hours of preliminary arrest had already expired for Marchica and were falling due for Arena and Pizzuco too. At nine o'clock sharp Marchica started pounding on the guard-room door to insist on his rights, of which he was well aware, and was told by the sergeant-major that the Public Prosecutor had extended his detention for another twenty-four hours. Marchica, more or less reassured as to the form, resigned himself to the substance, or the plank bed on which he lay down again with a certain relief. The sergeant-major left him, mulling over the fact that Marchica had started agitating exactly at nine o'clock when he had no watch, as this, together with his wallet, tie, belt and shoe-laces, were in a drawer of the office.

At ten o'clock the sergeant-major woke Marchica again and returned his belongings. Marchica thought he was about to be released; the combination of sleep, worry and stubble on his face broke into a triumphant grin. But outside the barracks was a car into which the sergeant-major shoved him. There was already one carabiniere in the back and another one followed Marchica, who found himself squeezed tight between two carabinieri in the back seat of a Fiat 600. He at once invoked the highway code, and the sergeant-major, already seated beside the driver, was so taken by surprise that he merely changed the subject with an amiable: 'Anyway, you're all thin.'

At C., Pizzuco and Arena were already in the cells of

65

the Carabinieri Company H.Q. The captain had thought that if he let them stew in their own juice for twenty-four hours, they would be riper for interrogation; a day and a night of discomfort were bound to have their effect on all three men.

He began with Marchica.

Company H.Q. was in an old convent, rectangular, each side with two rows of rooms divided by a corridor, one row with the windows facing inwards on to a court-yard, the other outwards on to the streets. To this unharmonious building the Sicilian statesman Francesco Crispi, and his even more harassed ministry, had added another, ugly and shapeless, which attempted to repro-duce, in smaller proportion, the original layout. The result was something like a child's copy of an engineer's design. In place of the courtyard there was a kind of shaft; and the two buildings were connected by a maze of passages and staircases which made it difficult to find one's way about until one knew them really well. It had, though, the advantage of providing larger rooms than the old building. The first floor was used as offices and the second as the C.O.'s quarters.

The C.O.'s office had a large window opening on to the shaft; opposite, with an equally large window, was his lieutenant's office, the two windows being so close that, by leaning out, papers could be passed from one to the other.

The desk was arranged for Marchica to sit facing the window, with the office door on his right.

'Were you born at B. ?' began the captain.

'Yes, I was,' replied Marchica in a tone of resignation.

'And have you always lived there ?'

'Not always. I've been in the army and done a few years in prison.'

'I suppose you know many people in B. ?'

'It's my home-town. But you know how it is, sometimes one's away for a couple of years; then one suddenly finds the boys grown up, the old people older. And as for the women ... You leave 'em as little girls playing with nuts in the street and, when you come back, find 'em with babies clinging to their skirts and maybe misshapen bodies ... '

'But those of our own age, who have always lived near us and played with us as kids, we recognize them at once, don't we?'

'Sure,' said Marchica, beginning to worry more about the captain's unruffled, conversational manner than the trend of his questions.

The captain was silent a moment as though absorbed in his own thoughts; and Marchica looked out of the window at the lieutenant's office opposite, empty and brightly lit. The captain had been careful to light only the table-lamp in his own office and it was turned down towards a little side-table where the sergeant was writing; thus Marchica had a perfect view of the other office.

'Then you must have known a man called Paolo Nicolosi ... '

'No,' said Marchica hastily.

'You must have,' said the captain. 'Maybe you don't remember him for the moment, as he left B. some years ago. I'll try to refresh your memory. Nicolosi used to live in Via Giusti which is a turning off Via Monti where you, if I'm not mistaken, have always lived ... His father was

67

a smallholder but worked as a tree-pruner; the son, now married and living in S., carries on the same job ... '

'Now you mention all this, I do seem to remember ... '

'Good ... After all, some things, some people; it's not so difficult to remember, particularly if they're associated with a happy period of one's life: childhood, for instance ... '

'We used to play together, I remember. But he was younger. And when I went to prison for the first time – unjustly, as truly as God is in the Sacrament – he was still a boy; I've never seen him since ... '

'What's he like? His face, I mean, his build ... ?'

'About my height, with fair hair and bluish eyes ... '

'A little moustache,' said the captain with conviction. 'He had one before ... '

'Before when?'

'Before ... before he shaved it off.'

'So you must have seen him when he had a moustache, then after he'd shaved it off.'

'Maybe I'm getting mixed up ... Now I come to think of it, I'm sure I am ... '

'No, you're not,' the captain reassured him, 'your memory's excellent. He wore a moustache until he got married, then he shaved it off. Maybe his wife didn't like it ... You must have met him at B., then. I don't know whether Nicolosi has been to B. lately, since you were let out under the amnesty, but it seems likely ... Or maybe you met him at S.?'

'I haven't been to S. for years.'

'That's odd,' said the captain, as though faced by an unexpected problem, 'very odd; for it was Nicolosi himself who said he'd met you at S. and I can't see any reason for him to lie about it … '

Marchica was floundering. The captain looked at him, gauging his bewilderment; to and fro under the midday August sun ranged Marchica's mind like a dog, exploring every possibility, every uncertainty and presentiment with the instinct of a hunted beast.

Suddenly the door of the office opened and Marchica automatically looked round to see who it was. In the doorway was the sergeant-major of S., who saluted and said: 'He's made up his mind.' Behind him, holding up his trousers, dishevelled and unshaven, stood Pizzuco. At a sign from the captain, the sergeant-major quickly closed the door and withdrew. Marchica was overwhelmed with dismay. There was no doubt about it, Pizzuco, after the flogging he had undergone, was going to spill the beans (actually Pizzuco had been dragged out of bed that minute, with nerves shattered by bad dreams, not by torture). Then under the naked light in the office opposite, Marchica saw Pizzuco, the lieutenant, and the sergeant-major enter, the lieutenant sit down and at once put a short question to Pizzuco. Pizzuco began talking away and the sergeant-major writing furiously. Actually the lieutenant had merely asked him about his means of livelihood; and Pizzuco was pouring out the edifying story of his honest and blameless existence based on indefatigable toil, all of which was being taken down by Sergeant-Major Ferlisi's nimble pen. But Marchica, in his inner ear, heard Pizzuco's voice revealing a story which, at the very best, meant a twenty-seven-year sentence for him, twenty-seven long years in the Ucciardone from which not even God could save him.

'What reason could there be to lie about it?' went on the captain. 'I don't mean you, I mean Nicolosi. What reason could he have had, to say something that's, after all, so petty, so unimportant?'

'He can't say it,' said Marchica firmly.

'And why not?'

'Because ... because he can't.'

'Perhaps it's because you think, rightly and with good reason, that Nicolosi's already dead ... '

'Dead or alive, it's all the same to me.'

'Well, no, you're right, you know. Nicolosi *is* dead.'

Visible relief showed on Marchica's face, a sign that, without the captain's confirmation, he would still have had some doubts whether Nicolosi was really dead or not. Therefore he was not the man who had killed Nicolosi.

(In the other office Pizzuco was muttering: 'You bastard, you yellow rat, you son of a sow. Four strokes of the cat and you spew up everything. You'll pay for it, though; either at my hands or someone else's, you'll pay!')

'Yes,' said the captain, 'Nicolosi is dead, but sometimes the dead talk, you know ... '

'Only at a spiritualist's table,' said Diego scornfully.

'No. They can talk by the simple method of writing something before they die. And Nicolosi, after meeting you, had the excellent idea of writing your name and nickname on a piece of paper: Diego Marchica known as *Zicchinetta*. He then added the time and place and the very plausible opinion that the presence of *Zicchinetta* at S. at that hour was connected with the killing of Colasberna ... Quite a letter, in fact ... which, seeing that Nicolosi is dead, will carry more weight with the

judges than any evidence he could have given alive ...
What a blunder you made! Nicolosi left the note with
his wife with instructions only to hand it over to us if
anything happened to him. If you'd let him live, I'm
certain he would never have dared give evidence, let
alone come forward and report what he had seen. It was
a fatal mistake, killing him ... '

In the opposite office Pizzuco had finished his
harangue; the sergeant-major put his sheaf of papers in
order, and came over to make him sign the sheets, one at
a time. Then the sergeant-major left the room and
appeared a moment later in the captain's office with some
sheets of paper under his arm. Marchica was sweating
blood.

'I don't know what you think of Rosario Pizzuco?'
said the captain.

'A sponge-full of slander,' said Diego.

'I'd never have believed it, but I agree with you. I
understand that, for you Sicilians, "slander" is the word
used for revealing actions that should never be revealed,
though they deserve the proper punishment of the law ...
I agree with you. Pizzuco has committed that kind of
"slander". Do you want to hear it? ... Read it out,' he
said to the sergeant, handing him the sheets which had
been brought in by the sergeant-major.

The forged statement, which had been very carefully
thought out, declared that, of his own free will ('flogging', thought Diego, 'flogging'), Rosario Pizzuco confessed to having met Marchica some time previously and
told him confidentially of insults that he had received
from Colasberna. Marchica had offered to avenge him;
but he, being Rosario Pizzuco, a man of sound moral

71

principles, allergic to any kind of violence and quite alien to vindictive feelings, had rejected the offer. Marchica had insisted, even blaming Pizzuco for his undignified attitude of forbearance in regard to Colasberna, adding that he, Marchica, also had personal motives for resentment against the same man, about a job or some money refused him by Colasberna, Pizzuco didn't quite remember which; and that, one of these days, he was going to *astutare* or 'snuff' Colasberna, meaning that he was going to snuff out his life as one snuffs a candle. This proposal he would doubtless have put into effect. But a day or two after Colasberna's murder, Pizzuco had gone to B. on a land deal, met Marchica by chance, and been told in confidence, without his even asking, an appalling story of a double murder. Marchica's exact words had been: 'I set off to snuff out one and found that I had to snuff out two,' which, in Marchica's underworld jargon, meant quite definitely that he had committed two murders: Colasberna, and the other, Pizzuco suspected, Nicolosi, whose disappearance was arousing comment. Pizzuco had been appalled at this dangerous revelation and gone home very upset. Of course, he had not mentioned the matter to a living soul, as, knowing Marchica's violent character, he'd feared for his own life. Asked why Marchica had confided such a dangerous secret to him, Pizzuco had replied that perhaps Marchica, who had been away from the district for a long time, thought he could take Pizzuco into his confidence owing to certain experiences in common – though only superficially so, added Pizzuco; both, during the confused period of the Separatist Movement, having served with the EVIS, the Volunteer

Army for Sicilian Independence, Pizzuco for the purest of idealistic motives, Marchica for his own criminal ends. To the further question whether it was possible to discern the hand of other persons, of instigators, that is, behind Marchica, Pizzuco had replied that he did not know but that, in his own opinion, this was quite out of the question; he simply attributed the crimes to the violent character and the overwhelming criminal urge to prey on others' lives and property of which Marchica had always given ample proof.

It was a masterly piece of forgery, a living portrait of men like Marchica and Pizzuco, and had been concocted by three sergeant-majors in collaboration. The wiliest touch was the last statement attributed to Pizzuco: the downright exclusion of complicity by a third party. To bring in the name of Mariano Arena would have struck a false note, and been too improbable; the whole card-castle would have come tumbling down under Marchica's suspicious analysis. But the technique of throwing all blame downwards, that is on to Marchica; the categorical denial of any on his own part; the rejection of any suggestion of a third party; all this made Marchica agonizingly certain that the statement was authentic. Not for one moment, in fact, did he doubt the voice of the sergeant which was now supplying the sound-track to that mute scene which he had watched through the window before.

Demoralized, blinded by a rage which, had he been able to lay hands on Pizzuco, would have meant the end of the latter's career of crime, he sat for a long while in silence. Then he said that, if that was the way things were, all he could do was what Samson did. 'Samson died,' he said, 'and so did all his companions' ('*Mori Sansuni cu tuttu lu cumpagnuni*'), by which he meant that he was going to put the facts narrated by that filthy son of a bitch in their proper light.

He had met Pizzuco for the first time in many years during the first week of December of the previous year at B. Pizzuco had suggested he should bump off Colasberna, who had mortally insulted him; the price, three hundred thousand lire. Marchica, who had only been out of prison for a month or so and wanted to enjoy a little freedom in peace, had said that he didn't feel like the job. Then, being broke, when Pizzuco insisted and flashed before his eyes the prospect of a cash payment on account and the rest on completion, promising him a job as an overseer into the bargain, he had yielded. Only because he was broke, mind you. Terrible being broke. So he and Pizzuco studied a plan of action; Pizzuco even promised to abet him by leaving the murder weapon for him in a house of Pizzuco's in the country where Marchica was to go the night before the killing. From this house, which was not far from town, Marchica was to follow an agreed route and take up a position at the corner of Via Cavour at the time the first bus left for Palermo, since Colasberna used to catch that bus every Saturday. Having pulled off the job, Marchica was to make a rapid get-away down Via Cavour and return to the house in the country, whence Pizzuco was to pick him up later with a car and drive him back to B.

A few days before the killing Marchica went to S. to reconnoitre and make sure that he could recognize Colasberna. On this occasion Pizzuco fixed the date for the murder.

74

On the sixteenth of January at six thirty a.m., following in every detail the plan devised by Pizzuco, Marchica killed Salvatore Colasberna. However, there had been one snag: while Marchica was running off down Via Cavour he had bumped into his fellow-townsman, Paolo Nicolosi, who evidently recognized him, since he called him by name. Marchica had been alarmed by this and when, shortly afterwards, Pizzuco came to pick him up at the house, he told him of the encounter. Pizzuco was thrown into a high state of alarm and began swearing; then, calming down, he said, 'Don't you worry, we'll fix it.' Pizzuco had then taken him in a small van to the Granci neighbourhood, just under a kilometre from B.; first, though, he had paid him one hundred and fifty thousand lire which, with the payment on account, made up the agreed three hundred thousand, and cleared the deal.

A day or so later Pizzuco came to B. and told Marchica that he need not worry about Nicolosi any more, as the latter, in Pizzuco's exact words, 'was only good for giving sugar dolls to children', a reference to a local custom, whereby, on All Souls' Day, children receive gifts of sugar dolls. From this expression Marchica was sure that Nicolosi had been eliminated.

Asked whether Pizzuco, when commissioning him to kill Colasberna, might have been acting on behalf of others, Marchica answered that he did not know, but he, personally, did not think so. Asked whether Pizzuco's remark: 'We'll fix it' did not imply the participation or help of others unknown to Marchica but accomplices of Pizzuco, Marchica repeated that he did not think so, and even went on to say that he could not really remember

75

whether Pizzuco had said: 'We'll fix it' or 'I'll fix it.' Asked if he had any idea where or how Nicolosi had been killed, he said he had none.

As he talked, Diego Marchica grew calmer. He nodded at the captain's reading of his confession, and signed it with satisfaction. Having fixed that swine Pizzuco – and incidentally himself – and having had the good manners not to involve others who were not swine, he felt at peace with his conscience and resigned to his fate. Maybe he was meant to spend the rest of his days in prison but, apart from the fact that he was used to it by now and for him it was rather like getting back home after a tiring journey, was not life itself rather a prison?

Life was all tribulation: lack of money, the temptation to play *zecchinetta*, the sergeant-major's searching eye, other people's good advice; and, work above all, the hell of having to do a day's work – work which degrades one to animal level. Enough of it all; better sleep on it. And indeed sleep, dark, amorphous, was again taking possession of all his thoughts.

The captain sent him off to sleep at the S. Francesco prison, in solitary; thus postponing until after the preliminary proceedings the rousing reception that Diego was bound to receive from his fellow jail-birds.

Now came Pizzuco's turn. It was already very late.

In other circumstances, Pizzuco would have aroused pity; stiff from chill and his arthritis, his eyes and nose dripping with a streaming cold, bewildered by what had happened to him, he was rolling his watery eyes in a blank stare, mouthing words as if unable to find his voice.

The captain had the sergeant read him Marchica's

confession. Pizzuco swore by the Holy Sacrament, before Christ on the Cross, on the souls of his mother, wife and son Giuseppe, that Marchica's was the blackest of slanders, and called down on him, until the seventh generation, the just vengeance of heaven where, apart from the other dead relatives already listed, he had an uncle praying for him, a canon who had died under suspicion, well-chosen word, of sanctity. In spite of his chill and misery, he was a brilliant speaker. His speech was thick with imagery, hyperbole and symbolism, couched in an Italianized Sicilian, sometimes more effective, sometimes more incomprehensible than pure dialect. The captain gave him his head for a while, then coldly observed:

'So you don't even know this Marchica?' – for that was what Pizzuco had seemed to be driving at during his long preamble.

'Oh, so far as that goes, I know him, Signor Capitano; though I'd better have been killed before I ever met him. I know him, and I know what he's like ... But we've never been at all close, and as for depriving a human being of life, heaven forbid! ... Never, Signor Capitano, never! For Rosario Pizzuco the life of a human being, any human being, is set on the high altar of a church; it's sacred, Signor Capitano, sacred ... '

'So you do know this Marchica, then?'

'I know him. Can I deny it? I know him, but it's as though I didn't. I know what sort of a man he is and have always steered clear of him.'

'And how d'you explain this confession of his?'

'Who can explain it? Maybe he's gone mad, maybe he wants to ruin me ... Who can tell what goes on in the mind of a man like that? ... His mind is like one of those sour pomegranates; every thought a grain of malice, enough to set the teeth of a man like me on edge with fright ... He's capable of killing out of hand just because someone doesn't say good morning or he takes a dislike to the way he laughs ... A born criminal ... '

'I see that you know his character very well.'

'I should think so, too. He's always crossing my path ... '

'How many times has he crossed your path of late? Try to remember.'

'Let's see ... I met him when he had just come out of prison; that's once ... Then I met him at B., his home-town; that's twice ... Then he came to S. and that was the third time ... Three times, Signor Capitano, three times.'

'And what did you talk about?'

'Nothing, Signor Capitano, nothing. Matters so trifling one forgets them at once, like writing on the waters of a well ... I congratulated him on being free again and thought: what a waste of an amnesty. I said I hoped he'd enjoy his liberty and thought: he'll soon be inside again; and we talked of the harvest, the weather, his friends, mere nothings.'

'According to you then, there's not a grain of truth in what Marchica says ... But, leaving Marchica out of it for the moment, we know with absolute certainty that about three months ago – I can give you the exact date if you want – you had a conversation with Salvatore Colasberna during which you made him certain offers, offers which Colasberna turned down, about ... '

'Advice, Signor Capitano, advice: just disinterested advice for friendship's sake ... '

'If you are in a position to give advice, you must be well-informed.'

'Well-informed? I pick things up here and there. My work gets me around. Today I hear one thing, tomorrow another ... '

'What had you heard that prompted you to give advice to Colasberna?'

'That his business was doing badly. I advised him to seek protection, help ... '

'From whom?'

'Oh, from friends, banks; by trying to get into the right political current ... '

'And which, according to you, is the right political current?'

'The government's, I'd say: who's in power lays down the law, and whoever wants to be in with the law should go along with the party in power.'

'So you had no definite advice to give Colasberna?'

'No, none, Signor Capitano.'

'Shall we say you just gave him some general advice, purely for friendship's sake?'

'Just so.'

'But you weren't all that friends with Colasberna.'

'Well, we knew each other ... '

'Do you always go out of your way to give advice to people you hardly know?'

'That's the way I am. If I see anyone in trouble, I'm always ready to give him a hand.'

'Did you ever give a hand to Paolo Nicolosi?'

'What's that got to do with it?'

'Having given a hand to Colasberna, it seems only natural to give one to Nicolosi.'

The telephone on the desk rang. As the captain listened to the message, he studied Pizzuco, who was now calmer and more sure of himself; even his nose had stopped dri͟ping.

Replacing the receiver, he said: 'Now let's start all over again.'

'All over again?'

'Yes. That call was from S. to tell me that the weapon which killed Colasberna has been found. D'you want to know where? ... No, don't blame your brother-in-law ... He was just going to carry out your instructions when the carabinieri arrived and arrested him. Late this evening he went into the country, got the sawn-off shotgun and was just going to get rid of it when the carabinieri showed up ... An unfortunate coincidence ... You know what your brother-in-law's like; he thought that all was up; he said he'd had instructions from you to hide the gun in the Gramoli *chiarchiaro* – on your orders, he said.' Turning to the sergeant, he asked: 'What is a *chiarchiaro*?'

'A stony part,' said the sergeant, 'a place full of caves, holes in the ground, ravines.'

'I thought as much,' said the captain, 'and I have an idea which may, or may not, be a good one. Might we find Nicolosi's body in the *chiarchiaro* too?' And he turned to Pizzuco with a frosty smile. 'What do you think of my idea?' he asked.

'It might be a good one,' said Pizzuco impassively.

'Well, if you approve, I feel quite safe,' said the captain; and he rang up the carabiniere station of S. to order a search made in the Gramoli *chiarchiaro*.

While he was telephoning, Pizzuco was hastily examining the best line to take. By the time the captain said: 'Now you can either confirm Marchica's story by confessing you gave him instructions to kill Colasberna and that you yourself killed Nicolosi; or you can exculpate Marchica by confessing that you killed both Colasberna and Nicolosi,' Pizzuco had already chosen a third alternative which was oddly like the forged statement that had made Marchica confess. It differed from it only on one point, in fact. The sergeant-majors who had elaborated the forged confession knew their business all right. They had the psychology of a man like Pizzuco weighed up with scientific precision. No wonder Diego Marchica had fallen like a capon into the pot.

Pizzuco now said that about three months previously he had met Colasberna and, out of the goodness of his heart, even though they had not been particular friends, had given him some advice on how to run his building concern. But instead of the expressions of gratitude which Pizzuco had expected, Colasberna had told him, in unrepeatable terms, to mind his own business and thank the Lord that he, Colasberna, had not made Pizzuco pick all his teeth up from the ground; those had been his exact words, meaning, of course, that he had not knocked them out for him. Pizzuco, a man of peace, who only got into unpleasant situations owing to his incurable kindness of heart, had been deeply grieved by this reaction of Colasberna's; he happened to mention it casually to Marchica, and the latter had offered to take vengeance, even without any reward on Pizzuco's part, as he too had a personal grudge against Colasberna. Pizzuco, horrified, had categorically rejected this offer. But some days later, Marchica came to S. and asked to be allowed to stay at a house in the country belonging to Pizzuco's wife in the Poggio district, near S. It was to be only for one night, as he had important business to do in S., a town which boasted no hotel. Marchica also asked him for the loan of a shotgun, as he'd heard that hares abounded in those parts and he wanted to do a bit of shooting early in the morning. Pizzuco gave him the key of the house, and told him he would find an old, a very old, shotgun there; it wasn't much good, but it might serve his purpose. Being of a trusting nature and always ready to do a good turn, he had had no inkling of the criminal plot Marchica was hatching. Not even after he had heard of Colasberna's death had his suspicions been aroused. Only when the carabinieri came to his house to arrest him had it dawned on him what a terrible predicament Marchica, taking advantage of his good faith, had plunged him into. So he gave his brother-in-law instructions to get rid of the gun which, it was clear by now, had been used by Marchica for illicit purposes. This had seemed to him the best course, for, owing to Marchica's vindictive nature, he had not dared reveal to the police the circumstances of which he was the victim.

*   *   *

'Oh, Excellency!' exclaimed His Excellency, leaping out of bed with an agility surprising in one of his age and decorum.

The ringing of the telephone had, with nagging persistency, infiltrated through sleep to his consciousness, and he had reached for the instrument with the sensation that his hand was detached from his body. As faint sounds and distant voices reached his ear, he switched on the light; this meant that his wife would have no more that night of the sleep which always came sparingly to her restless body.

Suddenly the faint sounds and distant voices fused into one single voice, still distant but irritated and inflexible; and His Excellency found himself out of bed, barefoot in his pyjamas, bowing and smiling as though bows and smiles were sliding down the mouthpiece.

His wife gave him a disgusted look and, before turning her splendid bare shoulders to him, muttered: 'He can't see you; there's no need to wag your tail.' Indeed, a tail was all His Excellency needed at that moment to express his devotion.

Again he said: 'Excellency!' then: 'but, Excellency ... no, Excellency ... yes, Excellency ... very well, Excellency,' and after saying 'Excellency' some hundred times, he stood there, telephone in hand, grunting comments about the mother of an Excellency who rang from Rome at two a.m. to upset his life. He looked at his wife's back. Wasn't she upsetting it enough already? He put the telephone down on its rest, then picked it up at once and dialled a number. His wife turned on him like a scalded cat: 'Tomorrow night I'm sleeping in the guest-room,' she snapped.

Now he was saying in the same irritated and inflexible tone he had listened to a few minutes before: 'I'm sorry, my friend, but I've just been woken up myself. I'm awake and you're awake and you'll kindly do me the favour of waking whoever you have to wake ... I've just had a call from Rome; I'm not saying from who, but you can guess ... That Bellodi – I told you, remember? – has stirred up scandal on a national scale ... National, I tell you ... One of those scandals that, when someone like you or I is involuntarily involved, means there's hell to pay, my friend, blackest hell ... D'you know what a Rome newspaper came out with this evening? ... No? Well, you're lucky. I had to hear it from the party concerned and, believe me, he was in a fury ... There was a half-page, blown-up photograph of ... you know who ... standing next to Don Mariano Arena ... What d'you think of that! A photo montage? Not on your life. A genuine photograph. You say you don't care? ... That's not a very bright reaction ... Yes, I know as well as you do that it's not our fault if His Excellency is ingenuous enough, let's call it that, to be photographed with Don Mariano ... Yes, I'm listening ... '

His wife bounded out of bed, ravishing in her nudity. Like a famous actress, in bed she wore only Chanel Number 5; thus arousing His Excellency's sensuality and dulling that bureaucratic ardour of his which had rendered such service in the days of the Salo Republic. Wrapped in an eiderdown and an aura of scorn, she swept out, followed by His Excellency's anxious glance.

'Very well, then,' he said, after listening for a couple of minutes, 'this is what we'll do: in the course of the night you'll either nail down this Don Mariano for me with proof that even God Almighty couldn't touch; or else, also in the course of the night, you'll turn him loose and the press can be told that he was merely held for questioning ... What! The Public Prosecutor is following the investigations and agrees with Bellodi? ... Hell, what a mess! ... Well, do something ... Yes, of course I realize ... But d'you know what he told me only a

moment ago? ... You know who ... He told me that
Don Mariano Arena is an honest citizen and that one of
us here, either me or you, is playing the communists'
game ... How ever did this Bellodi get here? Why the
devil did they send a man like that to an area like this?
What's needed here, my friend, is discretion; a good
nose, presence of mind, steady nerves, that's what's
needed ... And they send down someone with St Vitus's
dance ... But, for goodness' sake! that I don't question
for a moment ... I have the utmost respect for the
Service, I honour it ... Well, do whatever you want ... '
and he slammed down the receiver.

Now he had to calm his wife, a thornier problem than
the thorniest ever set by his job.

*   *   *

Dawn was infusing the countryside; it seemed to rise
from the tender green wheat, from the rocks and dripping
trees, and mount imperceptibly towards a blank sky. The
chiarchiaro of Gramoli, incongruous in green uplands,
looked like a huge, black-holed sponge soaking up the
light flooding the landscape. Captain Bellodi had reached
that point of exhaustion and sleeplessness which pro-
duces a series of incandescent fantasies: hunger does the
same; at a certain intensity it fades into a kind of lucid
starvation which rejects any idea of food. The captain
thought: 'This is where God throws in the sponge,'
associating the sight of the *chiarchiaro* with the struggle
and defeat of God in the human heart.

Partly joking, and partly because he knew the captain
to be interested in popular sayings, the sergeant said:

> '*E lu cuccu ci dissi a li cuccuotti:*
> *A lu chiarchiaru nni vidiemmu tutti.*'

The captain asked what it meant, his curiosity instantly aroused.

The sergeant translated: 'An owl said to its owlets: we'll all meet in the end at the *chiarchiaro*,' adding that perhaps this meant we shall all meet again in death, the *chiarchiaro* having in some way, who knew why, become associated with the idea of death. The captain knew why very well; and in his feverish imagination he saw a host of night birds in the *chiarchiaro*, an aimless flapping of wings in the pallid light of dawn. No image, he thought, could ever convey more fearsomely the impression of death.

They had left their car on the road and were now approaching the *chiarchiaro* down a narrow, muddy path. Carabinieri could be seen moving about the *chiarchiaro* and a peasant or two helping them.

Suddenly the path ended at a farmhouse; and they had to cross some fields of wheat to reach the sergeant-major of S., who could now be made out quite clearly, gesticulating as he directed operations.

When they were within earshot, the sergeant-major called with an exultation out of keeping with the discovery of a corpse: 'He's here all right, sir! It'll be a job to get 'im up, but he's here!' But this was his work, and the finding of a murdered man was grounds in this case for satisfaction and rejoicing.

It was there, the body; at the bottom of a thirty-foot cleft which had been sounded with a rope and stone as plumbline. The light of electric torches, filtering through bushes growing on the sides of the cleft, barely showed the bottom. But upwards wafted, unmistakably, the stench of putrefaction. To the great relief of the carabinieri, who were afraid the job would fall to one of them, a peasant had volunteered to go down tied to a rope and attach the body to other ropes so that it could be hauled up with comparative ease. A lot of rope was needed and they were waiting for the return of a cara- biniere who had gone to fetch it from the village.

The captain went back across the fields to the farm- house where the path began. It seemed deserted. But, going round to the side facing away from the *chiarchiaro*, a dog suddenly sprang towards him to the limit of its rope; it hung there, nearly choked, by its collar, barking furiously. It was a handsome brown mongrel with little violet half-moons over its yellow eyes. An old man came out of the cowshed to quieten it. 'Down, *Barruggieddu*, down!' he said, and then to the captain: 'I kiss your hands.'

The captain went over to the dog to stroke it.

'No,' said the old man in alarm, 'don't touch 'im, he's wicked! He'll let a stranger touch 'im and be reassured, and then bite 'im … He's a little devil.'

'What d'you call him?' asked the captain, wondering about the strange name the old man had used.

'*Barruggieddu*,' said the old man.

'What does that mean?'

'Someone who's bad,' said the old man.

'I've never heard that one before,' the sergeant said; then in dialect asked the old man for an explanation. The old man said that perhaps the right name was *Barricci- eddu* or maybe *Bargieddu* but, in any case, it meant

87

'evil', the evil of a man in a position of command. At one time the *Barruggieddi* or *Bargieddi* had lorded it over the townships and sent people to the gallows for their own cruel pleasure.

'I've got it,' said the captain. 'It means the Bargello – the chief of police.'

Embarrassed, the old man was mute.

The captain had wanted to ask him whether, a few days previously, he had noticed anyone going towards the *chiarchiaro* or had seen anything suspicious in those parts; but he realized that there was nothing to be got out of a man who considered a chief of police as evil as his own dog. Perhaps he wasn't so far wrong, thought the captain; for centuries the *bargelli* had bitten men like him, bitten after reassuring, as the old man had said. What had the *bargelli* been but tools of invading tyrants?

He took leave of the old man and set off down the path for the road. Straining at its rope, the dog barked its final menace. '*Bargello*,' thought the captain, '*bargello* like me, with my short length of rope, my collar, my mania,' and he felt more akin to the dog called *Barruggieddu* than to the historic *bargelli* of not so very long ago. 'Hound of the law,' he thought of himself; and then he went on to think of the 'hounds of the Lord', who were the Dominicans, and of the Inquisition, a word which conjured up a dark empty crypt and stirred gloomy echoes of history. He found himself wondering with anguish whether he, too, the fanatical hound of the law, had not already crossed the threshold of that crypt. Thoughts, thoughts born and melting in feverish self-destroying yearning for sleep.

He returned to C. and, before going to his quarters for a short rest, called in at the Public Prosecutor's office to report on the progress of his investigations and to extend the detention of Arena whom he wanted to interrogate in the afternoon after marshalling and assessing all his facts.

In the Palace of Justice, journalists were camping out on stairs and corridors. They were on him like a swarm of bees and the photographers' flashes exploded painfully into his arid-feeling eyeballs.

'How's the investigation going? ... Is Don Mariano Arena responsible for the murders or is there someone more important behind him? ... Have Marchica and Pizzuco confessed? ... Will their temporary arrest be extended or are there warrants out? ... D'you know anything about a tie-up between Don Mariano and Minister Mancuso? ... Is it true that the Honourable Member Livigni came to your office yesterday?'

'No, it isn't,' he replied to the last question.

'But politicians have intervened on behalf of Don Mariano, haven't they? Is it true that Minister Mancuso telephoned from Rome?'

'As far as I know,' he said in a loud voice, 'there has not been – nor can there be – any political intervention. As far as any connections between one of the detainees and certain politicians are concerned, all I know is what you've written yourselves. If such connections exist – and I don't wish to cast aspersions on your professional honesty – I have not, so far, had to take them into consideration or investigate them. Should these connections, in the course of my inquiries, become such as to draw the attention of the law, you can be sure that neither the Public Prosecutor nor myself will fail to do our duty ... '

This declaration was presented by an evening paper in a six-column headline as: 'Minister Mancuso also involved in Bellodi investigation.'

Evening papers come out, of course, by midday; and, by what in the South is lunch-time, the telephone wires were burning with the yells of those involved; yells which burst on the eardrums, sensitive enough at the best of times, of certain persons trying to drown their sorrows in the wines of Salaparuta or Vittoria.

* * *

'The problem is this: the carabinieri have three links of a chain in their hands. The first is Marchica, that they've grasped so firmly that it's like a ring for tying up mules set in a farmhouse wall.'

'Diego's not the sort to talk. He's got the guts of the devil.'

'Leave his guts out of this. The trouble with you is that you don't realize that a man who may be capable of killing ten, a thousand, a hundred thousand people, can also be a coward ... Diego, allow me to say so, has talked. So Pizzuco's link is now attached to his ... There are now two alternatives: if Pizzuco talks, there's the third link, Mariano's, joined to his; if he doesn't, he's still linked to Diego, but not very strongly, and a good lawyer could loosen that link without much trouble ... and in that case ... the chain comes to an end and Mariano is free.'

'Pizzuco won't talk.'

'I'm not so sure of that, my dear fellow. I always look on the blacker side of things, so let's suppose that Pizzuco does talk. If so, Mariano's for it. At a guess I'd say that at this moment the carabinieri are trying to weld Pizzuco's link to Mariano's. If it holds, two things can happen: either the chain ends with Mariano, or Mariano, old and ill as he is, decides to tell his beads ... In that case, my friend, the chain gets longer and longer, so long, in fact, that I and the minister and God Almighty get caught up in it ... A calamity, my good fellow, a calamity ... '

'You're talking like a skeleton at a feast ... Heavens alive, don't you know what kind of man Don Mariano is? Silent as the grave.'

'Yes, when he was young; now he's old with one foot in that grave of his. The flesh is weak, as Garibaldi said in his will, afraid that, in a moment of weakness, he might confess his sins to a priest, sins that must have been spiny as prickly pears. What I'm getting at is this: in a moment of weakness Mariano may break down and confess his sins, which, between ourselves, are not exactly few ... I had his dossier in my hands in 1927, it was thicker than that' – he pointed to one of Bentini's tomes – 'a kind of criminal encyclopedia ... a for arson, b for battery, c for corruption ... the lot. Fortunately the dossier vanished ... No, don't look at me like that; I'd no hand in it. Other friends, bigger fry than me, did the three-card trick with that dossier. From this office to that, from that to the other, until it vanished under the very nose of the Public Prosecutor, a terror, I recall. He flew right off the handle, I remember, threats right and left, and those who were under the deepest suspicion were those who had nothing to do with it, poor things. Then the Public Prosecutor was transferred elsewhere and the storm passed. The truth of the matter is this: Attorney-Generals, Public Prosecutors, judges, officers, chiefs of police, corporals of carabinieri, they all pass ... '

'Corporals! I like that!'

'There's nothing to laugh at, my good fellow. I hope with all my heart that your face never gets impressed on the memory of a corporal ... Anyhow, even corporals pass and we stay ... a jolt or two, an occasional scare, but we're still here.'

'But Don Mariano ... ?'

'Don Mariano, too, has had his little jolt, his little scare.'

'But he's still inside. What he must be going through ... '

'He's not suffering physically at all. If you imagine that they are keeping him tied on top of two drawers or giving him electric shocks, forget it. All that sort of thing's in the past; nowadays even carabinieri have to obey the law ... '

'The law be damned! Only three months ago ... '

'Forget it; we're talking about Don Mariano. Nobody would dare lay a finger on him, a man who's respected, enjoys protection, a man who can afford to pay for defence lawyers like De Marsico, Porzio and Delitala, the lot ... Certainly he'll have a bit of hardship to put up with. The guard-room isn't exactly a grand hotel: its plank bed is hard, its bucket stinks and he'll miss his coffee. Poor old fellow, he used to drink a strong double every half-hour ... But in a few days they'll let him out, shining with innocence like the Archangel Gabriel. And his life will settle down again and his affairs will go on prospering ... '

'A moment ago you were being alarmist, making me give up hope; now ... '

'A moment ago it was heads; now it's tails. I say tails should come up and things go well; but it just might come up heads.'

'We must see it's tails.'

'Well, then, listen carefully to my advice. We must pull the first ring out of that wall, we must get Diego freed.'

'Only if he wasn't the one to commit the disgrace ... '

'Even if he was, get him out. Let the investigation go ahead – it's in the hands of those two polenta-eaters anyway and no one can stop it. Let it go ahead, let it finish, let it all come before the Examining Magistrate and, meanwhile, prepare for Diego such a cast-iron alibi that anybody who tries to bite it will break his teeth.'

'How d'you mean?'

'I mean that on the day Colasberna was killed, and at the very same hour, Diego was a thousand miles from the scene of the crime, and in the company of highly respectable persons without a police record among them, honest men whose word no judge'd have the right to doubt.'

'But if he's confessed ... ?'

'If he's confessed, he must take back all he's said: declare that either under physical or moral torture – there are moral tortures too – he made statements to the carabinieri which do not correspond to the truth. The proof that these statements are quite untrue, sheer fantasy, is that certain persons of the utmost integrity

93

bear witness to the material impossibility of Diego having committed the crime. Only saints possess the gift of bi-location and I doubt whether any judge would credit Diego with sanctity ... Now just take a look at this newspaper, this little item of news: "In the S. murder cases, one line of inquiry has been neglected by the carabinieri ... " '

*   *   *

Captain Bellodi was reading about the line of inquiry which the Sicilian paper – usually extremely cautious and not at all addicted to criticisms of the 'forces of law and order' – had accused him of neglecting. This line, of course, was 'passion'; which might, to one conversant with the facts so far revealed by the inquiry, explain one of the crimes, but, in doing so, leave the other two in utter mystery. Perhaps the journalist, when visiting S., had gone to Don Ciccio the barber for a shave and been excited by that story of an affair between Nicolosi's wife and Passerello. In short, as a good journalist and Sicilian, what he said was: *cherchez la femme*. The captain's opinion was that police in Sicily should be given strict instructions not to *cherchez la femme*; for she was always found in the end, much to the detriment of justice.

In Sicily, thought Captain Bellodi, the *crime passionnel* is not the result of genuine passion, a passion of the heart, but of a sort of intellectual passion, an almost juridical concern for forms; juridical in the sense of the abstractions to which law is reduced at various levels of our legal system until they reach that formal transparency in which 'merit', that is, the human element, no longer

94

counts. Once this is eliminated, law simply reflects itself. A character by the name of Ciampi in Pirandello's *Cap of Bells*, for instance, talked as though he had the entire High Court of Appeal in plenary session in his mouth, so carefully did he eviscerate and reconstitute form, never even touching on 'merit'. Bellodi had come across a Ciampi in the early days of his service at C. Just like Pirandello's character, he had turned up in his office, not in search of an author (he already had a most illustrious one) but of a subtle recorder of his evidence; so, fearing the sergeant might be unable to grasp his intricate arabesques, he had insisted on speaking to an officer.

All this, thought the captain, is the result of the fact that the only institution in the Sicilian conscience that really counts, is the family; counts, that is to say, more as a dramatic juridical contract or bond than as a natural association based on affection. The family is the Sicilian's State. The State, as it is for us, is extraneous to them, merely a *de facto* entity based on force; an entity imposing taxes, military service, war, police. Within the family institution the Sicilian can cross the frontier of his own natural tragic solitude and fit into a communal life where relationships are governed by hair-splitting contractual ties. To ask him to cross the frontier between family and State would be too much. In imagination he may be carried away by the idea of the State and may even rise to being Prime Minister; but the precise and definite code of his rights and duties will remain within the family, whence the step towards victorious solitude is shorter.

While waiting for Arena to be brought to his office,

Captain Bellodi pondered these matters, in which literature offered his short experience sometimes the right, and sometimes the wrong, card. And his thoughts were just moving on to the mafia, and how it fitted into this pattern he had just been tracing, when the sergeant showed in Don Mariano Arena.

Before appearing in front of the captain, Don Mariano had demanded a barber and been given a refreshing shave by a carabiniere. Now he was stroking his face and luxuriating in the absence of a sandpapery beard which had caused him more worry than his own thoughts during the past two days.

The captain said: 'Please sit down.' Don Mariano sat down, gazing at the captain steadily from under his heavy lids: an inexpressive stare suddenly interrupted by a movement of the head, as if some mechanism had flicked the pupils upwards and inwards.

The captain asked him whether he had ever had any connection with Calogero Dibella, known as *Parrinieddu*. Don Mariano asked what he meant by connection: simple acquaintance, friendship or common interests?

'Take your choice,' said the captain.

'Truth is one. There's no choice: simple acquaintance.'

'And what was your opinion of him?'

'He seemed sensible enough. A youthful slip or two; but lately he seemed to be going straight.'

'Did he work?'

'You know about that better than I do.'

'I want to hear about it from you.'

'If you mean work with a spade, which was what his father brought him up to, Dibella worked as hard as you or I ... Maybe he worked with his brains.'

'And how d'you think he used his brains?'

'I don't know and I don't want to.'

'Why not?'

'Because I'm not interested: Dibella went his way and I mine.'

'Why d'you talk of him in the past tense?'

'Because he's been killed ... I heard an hour before you sent the carabinieri to my home.'

'It was Dibella himself, as a matter of fact, who sent the carabinieri to your home.'

'You're trying to muddle me.'

'No. I'll show you what Dibella wrote a few hours before his death,' and he showed Don Mariano a photostat copy of the letter.

Don Mariano took it and studied it at arm's length. He saw better from a distance, he said.

'What d'you think of it?' asked the captain.

'Nothing,' said Don Mariano, handing back the photograph.

'Nothing?'

'Less than nothing.'

'Doesn't it look like an accusation?'

'Accusation?' said Don Mariano in amazement. 'To me it doesn't look like anything. Just a piece of paper with my name on it.'

'There's another name as well.'

'Yes: Rosario Pizzuco.'

'D'you know him?'

'I know the whole town.'

'But Pizzuco in particular?'

'Not in particular. Like many others.'

'Did you have business dealings with Pizzuco?'

97

'Let me ask you a question. What kind of business d'you think I do?'

'Most kinds.'

'I'm not in business. I live on my income.'

'From where?'

'Land.'

'How many hectares d'you own?'

'Twenty-two *salme* and ... let's call it ninety hectares.'

'Do they pay well?'

'Not always; it depends on the year.'

'On average, what does a hectare of your land yield?'

'Much of my land is left to grass, for pasture ... I can't tell you how much a hectare of fallow land yields. I can tell you how much the sheep on it bring in ... Roughly half a million lire ... The rest is in wheat, beans, almonds and oil, depending on the year ... '

'How many hectares are under cultivation?'

'Fifty or sixty.'

'Then I can tell you how much a hectare yields: not less than a million lire.'

'You're joking!'

'No, it's you that's joking ... You tell me that, apart from your land, you have no other source of income and no interests in industry or commerce ... And I believe you. So I have to suppose that those fifty-four millions which you deposited in various banks last year, not withdrawn from previous deposits in other banks, represent the income from your land. A million per hectare ... I must confess, though, that it astounded an agricultural expert I consulted; according to him no land in these parts yields a net income of over a hundred thousand lire per hectare. D'you think he's mistaken?'

'No, he's not,' said Don Mariano, looking glum.

'We started off on the wrong foot, then ... Let's go back again. What are your sources of income?'

'No, we're not going back, not at all. I do what I like with my own money, move it about as I like ... I can say, though, that I don't always keep it in the bank. Sometimes I make loans to friends, without promissory notes, on trust ... Last year all the money I lent was repaid: so I made those deposits in banks ... '

'Where there were already other deposits, in your name and your daughter's ... '

'It's a father's duty to think of his children's future.'

'Very proper. And you have assured your daughter a life of ease ... But I'm not so sure your daughter would approve of the way you provided her with it ... I know that at the moment she's at a finishing-school in Lausanne – a very expensive, very famous one ... I expect, when you next see her, you'll find her very changed; more refined, pitying what you despise, respecting what you don't.'

'Leave my daughter out of this,' cried Don Mariano, with a spasm of rage. Then he relaxed, as if reassured, and said: 'My daughter's like me.'

'Like you? I hope not; and what's more, you're doing all you can so that she won't be, so that she'll be different ... And when your own daughter's so different that you can no longer recognize her, you'll have paid, in a way, the price of wealth acquired by violence and fraud.'

'You're sermonizing.'

'You're right: you go to church for a sermon, and here you expect to find a policeman: you're right ... So let's talk about your daughter from the point of view of what she costs you in hard cash, and of the money you've accumulated in her name. A great deal, a very great deal of money, of, shall we say, doubtful origin ... Look at these: they are photostat copies of the accounts in your own and your daughter's name at various banks. As you can see, we didn't just check at local branches: we went as far as Palermo ... A great deal, a very great deal of money: can you explain its origin?'

'Can you?' asked Don Mariano impassively.

'I'm going to try. Because it's in the money you so mysteriously accumulate that lie the motives for the crimes I'm investigating; these motives have to be more or less illustrated in my report on you for instigation to murder. I'm going to try ... but in any case you'll have to give an explanation to the income-tax authorities, as we'll be handing over all these data to them.'

Don Mariano shrugged his shoulders.

'We also have a copy of your income-tax returns and of your file at the Inland Revenue Office: you returned an income ... '

'The same as mine,' interrupted the sergeant.

' ... and your taxes came to ... '

'Slightly less than mine,' said the sergeant.

'You see,' said the captain, 'you have quite a bit of explaining to do.'

Don Mariano shrugged again.

'This is the moment when one ought to put on the screw,' thought the captain. 'It's no good trying to catch a man like this with the penal code. There'll never be enough evidence; the silence of both the honest and dishonest will always protect him. It's useless as well as dangerous to consider the chance of a suspension of constitutional rights. A new Mori would immediately become a political-electoral instrument; not of the government, but of a faction of the government: the Mancuso-Livigni one or the Sciortino-Caruso one. We ought to do here what they do in America: grab them for tax-evasion. But not only people like Mariano Arena; and not only in Sicily. There should be a swoop made on the banks, experts set to work on the books, falsified as often as not, of businesses big and small; the register of landed property brought up to date; a check should be made on all those of dubious character, young and old, who spend so much of their time and breath on politics; and on the company kept by the more restless members of the great family group which is the government; and on their families' neighbours, and their families' enemies, and on the luxury villas, custom-built cars, the wives and mistresses of certain civil servants; and their tenor of life compared to their salaries. Then the proper conclusions should be drawn. That's the only way men like Don Mariano can feel the ground begin to give way under their feet ... In any other country in the world a tax-evasion like this one, of which I have the proof, would be severely punished; here Don Mariano just laughs, knowing how little it will take to confuse the issue ... '

'I see the income-tax people don't worry you much.'

'I never worry,' said Don Mariano.

'How's that?'

'I'm not a well-read man: but there's one or two things I do know, and they're enough for me: the first is that we have a mouth under our noses – for eating more than talking ... '

'I have a mouth too,' said the captain, 'but I can assure you that with it I eat only what you Sicilians call "Government bread".'

'I know, but you're a man.'

'And what about the sergeant?' asked the captain ironically, pointing to Sergeant D'Antona.

'I don't know,' said Don Mariano, scrutinizing him with what, for the sergeant, was unwelcome attention. 'I,' went on Don Mariano, 'have a certain experience of the world; and what we call humanity – all hot air, that word – I divide into five categories: men, half-men, pigmies, arse-crawlers – if you'll excuse the expression – and quackers. Men are very few indeed; half-men few, and I'd be content if humanity finished with them ... But no, it sinks even lower, to the pigmies who're like children trying to be grown-ups, monkeys going through the motions of their elders ... Then down even lower we go, to the arse-crawlers who're legion ... And, finally, to the quackers; they ought to just exist, like ducks in a pond: their lives have no more point or meaning ... But you, even if you nail me to these documents like Christ to His Cross, you're a man.'

'So are you,' said the captain, not without emotion. Then, with a twinge of discomfort at having exchanged a 'Present Arms' with a head of the mafia, he tried to justify this by remembering that he had once shaken hands with Minister Mancuso and the Honourable Member Livigni as representatives of the people, surrounded by fanfares and flags amid the din of a National Holiday. Unlike them, Don Mariano, at least, was a man. Beyond the pale of morality and law, incapable of pity, an unredeemed mass of human energy and of loneliness, of instinctive, tragic will. As a blind man pictures in his mind, dark and formless, the world outside, so Don Mariano pictured the world of sentiment, legality and normal human relations. What other notion could he have of the world, if, around him, the word 'right' had always been suffocated by violence, and the wind of the world had merely changed the word into a stagnant and putrid reality?

'Why am I a man, not a half-man or even a quacker?' he asked with harsh exaggeration.

'Because,' said Don Mariano, 'in your position it's easy to trample on a man's face; but you treat it with respect ... Many years ago I had to take a mortal insult from men sitting where you and the sergeant are sitting now. An officer like you slapped me; and, down in the guard-rooms, a sergeant-major pressed his cigar-butt on the soles of my feet, and laughed ... I ask you: can a man sleep after such insults?'

'So I don't insult you?'

'No, you're a man,' repeated Don Mariano.

'And d'you consider it manly to kill or have killed another man?'

'I've never done anything of the sort. But if, just to pass the time of day, discussing life, you were to ask whether it was right to take someone's life, I'd say: it depends whether he's a man.'

'Was Dibella a man?'

'He was a quacker,' said Don Mariano with scorn. It was a slip. Words are not like dogs which can be whistled back to heel.

'Have you any particular reason for so classifying him?'

'None. I scarcely knew him.'

'Even so, your judgment is perfectly correct. You must have had some grounds ... Perhaps you knew he was a spy, an informer of the carabinieri ... '

'I didn't bother.'

'But you knew?'

'The whole town knew.'

'So much for our secret sources,' said the captain ironically, turning to glance at the sergeant. 'And if Dibella did sometimes do his friends a good turn by passing us on selected information ... What would you say?'

'No idea.'

'But on one occasion at least, some ten days ago, Dibella did let slip some genuine information: in this office and sitting where you're sitting now ... How did you get to know about it?'

'I didn't: and if I had, I wouldn't have been interested.'

'Maybe Dibella came and confessed his mistake to you from remorse ... ?'

'He was the sort to feel fear, not remorse. And there was no reason for him to come to me.'

'Are you the kind to feel remorse?'

'Neither remorse nor fear: never.'

'Some of your friends say you're very religious.'

'I go to church, I send money to orphanages ... '

'Do you think that's enough?'

'Of course it is; the Church is great because each can be in it according to his own lights.'

'Have you ever read the Gospels?'

'I hear them read out every Sunday.'

'What do you think of them?'

'Beautiful words: the Church is all beautiful.'

'For you, I see, beauty has nothing to do with truth.'

'Truth is at the bottom of a well: look into it and you see the sun or the moon; but if you throw yourself in, there's no more sun or moon: just truth.'

The sergeant was getting bored. He felt like a game-dog compelled to follow the trail of a hunter over arid stony ground without the faintest scent of game. A long, twisting trail. Murder had hardly been mentioned when the field suddenly broadened: the Church, humanity, death. Club conversation, God Almighty, and with a crook ...

'You have helped many a man to find truth at the bottom of a well,' said the captain.

Don Mariano stared at him with eyes cold as nickel coins. He made no reply.

'And Dibella had already found truth,' the captain went on, 'when he wrote your name and Pizzuco's.'

'Truth? Madness, you mean!'

'He was *not* mad ... I sent for him immediately after Colasberna's death: I'd already had anonymous information which enabled me to connect the murder with certain interests ... I knew that Colasberna had had proposals and threats and even been shot at, just as a warning. I asked Dibella if he could give me any information as to the identity of the person who had made those proposals and threats. Caught on the hop, but not enough to give me the right answer there and then, he gave me two names: one of the two just to confuse me, so I later found out ... I wanted to protect him; but I couldn't arrest both the men mentioned by him. I had to be sure of arresting the right one. Since they belonged to rival *cosche*, one of the two was in the clear; either La Rosa or Pizzuco ... Meanwhile, the disappearance of Nicolosi was reported. And I was surprised at certain coincidences ... Nicolosi, before disappearing, had left a name too. We pulled in a man called Diego Marchica, whom you must know, and he confessed ... '

'Diego?' burst out Don Mariano incredulously.

'Diego,' confirmed the captain; then he told the sergeant to read out his confession.

Don Mariano followed the reading with heavy breathing that sounded like asthma; actually it was anger.

'Diego, as you see, led us to Pizzuco without much trouble; and Pizzuco to you ... '

'No, not even God will lead you to me,' said Don Mariano with assurance.

'You have a high opinion of Pizzuco,' observed the captain.

'I've a high opinion of nobody, but I know 'em all.'

'I don't wish to disillusion you about Pizzuco, especially after Diego let you down so badly.'

'He's a cuckold,' said Don Mariano, his face twisted with a spasm of uncontrollable nausea. It was an unexpected sign of yielding.

'Don't you think you're being rather unfair? Diego never even mentioned you.'

'What have I to do with it?'

'If you've nothing to do with it, why are you so angry?'

'I'm not angry: I'm just sorry about Pizzuco, who's a decent person ... I'm always upset by disgrace.'

'You can guarantee that what Marchica says about Pizzuco is quite untrue?'

'I can guarantee nothing, not even a one-cent IOU.'

'But you don't think Pizzuco's guilty?'

'No, I don't.'

'And suppose Pizzuco himself had confessed, and named you as accomplice?'

'I'd say he'd gone out of his mind.'

'So it wasn't you who instructed Pizzuco to settle Colasberna, by fair means or foul?'

'No.'

'Have you any investments or interests in building companies?'

'I? Heavens no.'

'Didn't you recommend the Smiroldi company for a big contract, which was obtained by somewhat unorthodox methods, to say the least, thanks to your recommendation?'

'No ... Yes, but I make thousands of recommendations.'

'Of what kind?'

'All kinds: about contracts, jobs in banks, school examinations, government grants ... '

'And to whom do you address these recommendations of yours?'

'To friends who get things done.'

'Who in particular?'

'Whoever is friendliest and can do the most.'

'But don't you yourself get anything out of it, any profit, any token of thanks?'

'Just goodwill.'

'Sometimes, though ... '

'Sometimes I'm given a *cassata* for Christmas.'

'Or a cheque: Martini, the accountant of the Smiroldi

firm, remembers a substantial cheque made out to you and signed by Smiroldi himself; the cheque passed through his hands ... Maybe it was a token of thanks for landing an important contract, or had you done something else for the firm?'

'I don't remember: it could well have been a repaid loan.'

'Well, if you don't remember, we'll subpoena Smiroldi.'

'Fine: then I needn't try and remember. I'm old and my memory sometimes sticks.'

'May I just call on your memory about a more recent matter?'

'Let's see what it is.'

'The contract for the Monterosso-Falcone road. You managed to raise the money for an utterly useless road, on a quite impossible plan. That it was you who raised the money is shown by an article of a local correspondent who gave you the credit for it. Apart from this, doesn't the Fazello company also owe the award of a contract to your influence? That was what Signor Fazello told me, and he had no reason to lie.'

'He hadn't.'

'Has he, under any form whatsoever, shown you any gratitude?'

'Yes, he has! He came here and blabbed the whole story: he's paid me back, all right, with interest!'

* * *

An hour before the session was to begin they had collected their invitation cards from the Via della

Missione entrance. They had strolled in the arcade, had a coffee at Berardo's and paused to look at the illustrated weeklies hanging up on the bookstalls. Rome lay in enchantment under a gentle flow of sun and, sauntering along, they were hardly aware of the rush of traffic and the long-drawn-out screech of the trolley-buses. Voices, newsboys' voices shouting the name of their home-town coupled with the word 'crimes', sounded distant and unreal. They had been away from home for two days and had already spoken to two eminent criminal lawyers, a minister, five or six deputies and three or four men wanted by the police who were enjoying the golden idleness of Rome in the taverns and cafés of Testaccio. They felt at ease, and the invitation of their Member of Parliament to visit Montecitorio for a session in which the Government was to reply to questions about public order in Sicily seemed an ideal way to end a hectic day. The evening papers said that the temporary arrest of Marchica, Pizzuco and Arena had been converted into real arrest, since the Public Prosecutor had issued warrants. From what journalists had been able to glean, Marchica had confessed to one murder and attributed another to Pizzuco; Pizzuco had admitted his involuntary complicity in two murders committed by Marchica; two, not, as Marchica had confessed, one; and Arena had admitted nothing, nor had Marchica and Pizzuco accused him of any complicity. Even so, the Public Prosecutor had issued warrants against Marchica for premeditated murder, against Pizzuco for premeditated murder and instigation to murder and against Arena for instigation to murder. An ugly situation but, seen from Rome at an hour which bestowed on the city the gay, airy freedom of a soap-bubble, luminous, iridescent with colours of shop-windows and women's dresses, those arrest-warrants seemed to float upwards, light as kites, to whirl like a merry-go-round over the top of the Antonine column.

It was almost time. The two went down the subway and, amid the multicoloured throng more vivid under the crude neon of display windows, their subfusc overcoats, their faces, swarthy as the patron saint of S., their mourning bands, their language of nudges and exclamatory looks with which they noted and acclaimed the passing of a pretty woman, their hurried gait, attracted momentary interest. Most people took them for plainclothes men following a pickpocket. Really they were a glimpse of the problem of the South.

At the House, the ushers looked at them with misgiving, passed their invitation cards to and fro, asked for their identity cards and made them take off their overcoats. Eventually they were escorted to a box. It was just like a theatre, but the proscenium was quite different. They were looking over the rim of what seemed a huge funnel, at the bottom of which was a mass of dark suits in ant-like movement. There was the same light which in their parts heralded a storm, when clouds driven by winds from the Sahara roll up in a slow surge, filtering light through sand and water: a strange light which makes surfaces look like satin.

It took a little time before the abstract concepts of left, centre and right applied to the concrete topography of the House and to the more familiar party faces. When Togliatti's face emerged from behind a newspaper, they realized they were looking at the left; then, with the slow precision of a compass, they swung their gaze towards the centre, paused for a moment on the face of Nenni, on that of Fanfani, and came to rest on the member to whom they owed the spectacle. He seemed to be looking at them too and they waved but, lost in his own thoughts, he did not notice. What impressed them most was the constant coming and going of messengers from bench to bench, like shuttles imparting to the hall the mechanical movement of a loom. A hum of low persistent talk rose which seemed to come from an empty vault rather than from the groups of persons sitting on the amphitheatre benches, haggard and absorbed.

Every now and then a bell rang. Then a voice began to float on that sandy light, spreading like a patch of oil over the gradually increasing murmur of the hall. They were unable to locate the source of this voice until their eyes travelled down from the President of the Assembly, who was ringing the bell, to what, when present, must have been the Government bench, where they saw, sitting near the man speaking, Minister Pella.

'We want the Minister of the Interior!' shouted the benches on the left.

The President rang the bell. He said that the Minister of the Interior was prevented from coming, that the Undersecretary was there, which amounted to the same thing, that they should let him speak and that he was sure nobody would be lacking in respect for the House. He might have saved his breath.

'The Minister! the Minister!' the left continued shouting.

'Let 'im speak for Christ's sake,' said one of the two Sicilian spectators in his companion's ear.

They let him speak.

The Undersecretary said that as regards public order in Sicily the Government saw no particular reason for concern.

A howl of protest rose from the left. This was just subsiding when a voice from the right shouted: 'Twenty years ago in Sicily one could sleep with one's door open!'

The left and a part of the centre rose to their feet, yelling. The two leant over the rail to see the fascist beneath them who, in a voice like a bull's, was bellowing: 'Yes, twenty years ago there was order in Sicily; but it's been destroyed by you!' He pointed an accusing finger from Fanfani to Togliatti.

The two saw his shaven head and accusing finger and muttered in chorus: 'The order of horns on your head!'

A long, frenzied ringing of the bell: then the Undersecretary continued. About the happenings at S., to which the Honourable Members had referred in their question, the Government, he said, had no comment to make, since there was a judicial inquiry in course. The Government, however, considered these happenings as manifestations of normal criminality and rejected the interpretation put on them by the said Honourable Members. Furthermore, the Government indignantly rejected the base insinuation, spread by left-wing newspapers, that certain Members of Parliament – and even of the Government – had any connection whatsoever with elements of the so-called mafia, which, in the opinion of the Government, only existed in the imaginations of socialists and communists.

From the left-wing benches, now packed with deputies, rose a storm of protest. A tall, grey, hairless member left his bench and advanced to the Government's until stopped by three ushers. The insults he was shouting at the Undersecretary were such that the two spectators thought: 'This'll end with knives!' The bell rang frenziedly. Darting from the right like a cicada, the shaven-headed member reached the middle of the hall; other ushers rushed to restrain him as he hurled his insults towards the left. The word 'cretin' whizzed around him, grazing his massive head as Red Indians' arrows did Buffalo Bill's.

'They need a battalion of carabinieri here,' thought the two, admitting for the first time in their lives that carabinieri might have some use.

They looked down towards their friend, the Honourable Member. He was quite unperturbed. Noticing their look, he waved with a smile.

*   *   *

It was a languorous evening in Parma, touched by a melting light embracing memory, distance, indefinable tenderness. Steeped in a dimension already reflected in memory, Captain Bellodi was pacing the streets of his native city; but uppermost in his mind was the thought of far-off Sicily, with its burden of injustice and death.

He had been ordered to Bologna to attend a trial as recorder of evidence and, when the trial ended, had not felt like returning to Sicily at once; the prospect of a leave in Parma with his family was particularly sweet to one in his state of nervous strain. He had applied for sick-leave and been given a month.

Now, almost half-way through his leave, he had just

learnt, from a bundle of local newspapers sent by the enterprising Sergeant D'Antona, that his whole pains-taking reconstruction of the S. case had collapsed like a card-castle under a puff of irresistible alibis, of one alibi in particular, Diego Marchica's. Persons above all suspicion, highly respected for position and education, had borne witness to the sheer impossibility of Diego shooting Colasberna and being recognized by Nicolosi, as on the day and at the time the crime was committed Diego had been no fewer than seventy-six kilometres away: this was the exact distance, in fact, from S. to P., where Diego, in Doctor Baccarella's garden and under the very eyes of the doctor himself, who was in the habit of getting up early to supervise work in his garden, had been engaged in the harmless and peaceful task of hosing. This testimony could be confirmed not only by the doctor, but by peasants and passers-by, sure as they all were of Diego's identity.

The confession he had made to Captain Bellodi, Diego had explained, was due to a sort of spite; the captain had made him think that he had been incriminated by Pizzuco and, maddened by rage, he had tried to get even; just to put Pizzuco on the spot he had incriminated himself. Pizzuco on his part, confronted with Diego's treachery, had spouted a regular firework display of lies just to tie a millstone round Diego's neck for having incriminated him. The gun? Well, Pizzuco was certainly guilty of illicit possession of firearms; but it was this very worry about the weapon being illegal that had made him tell his brother-in-law to get rid of it.

As for Don Mariano, who had been much photographed and interviewed by the press, it goes without

saying that the patient web of clues woven by the captain
and the Public Prosecutor had melted into thin air. An
aura of innocence illuminated that ponderous head
which, even in photographs, wore an expression of wise
cunning. To a journalist who had asked him about
Captain Bellodi, Don Mariano had replied: 'He's a
man.' When the journalist asked whether by this Don
Mariano meant that like all men he was fallible, or
whether on the other hand there was an adjective missing, Don Mariano had said: 'Adjective be damned! A
man doesn't need adjectives and, if I say the captain's a
man, he's a man and that's all there is to it!' – a reply
considered by the journalist as sybilline, surely dictated
by anger and probably by rancour. Don Mariano,
however, had wished to express an objective appreciation,
like a victorious general praising a defeated adversary.
And so a note of ambiguity, of pleasure mingled with
irritation, was added to the turmoil of Captain Bellodi's
feelings.

Other items in the paper, marked in red by Sergeant
D'Antona, announced that, of course, the investigations
on the three murders had all been reopened, and that the
mobile police squad were well on the way to solving the
Nicolosi case and had arrested his widow and her lover,
a certain Passarello, a man under the 'darkest' suspicion;
it was inexplicable, the paper added, how this trail had
been overlooked by Captain Bellodi. Another red-
marked item, on the page devoted to news from the
province, stated that the commander of the carabiniere
station of S., Sergeant-Major Class 1 Arturo Ferlisi,
had, at his own request, been transferred to Ancona.
In a viaticum of good wishes and congratulations the

correspondent of the newspaper paid tribute to his equilibrium and ability.

Brooding over this news and seething with impotent rage, the captain was stalking aimlessly around the streets of Parma with the air of a man afraid of being late for an appointment. He did not even hear his friend Brescianelli call him by name from the opposite pavement and was surprised and annoyed when the other caught up and stopped him, standing, smiling affectionately and claiming at least a hand-shake in the name of their happy but, alas, distant schooldays. Bellodi gravely apologized for not hearing and told him that he wasn't feeling very well, forgetting that Brescianelli was a doctor. The other in fact took a step back to get a better look at him and noticed that he was thinner, as his overcoat hung too loosely from his shoulders; then he came nearer, took a look at his eyes which, he said, had a touch of burnt sienna in them, sign of liver-trouble, asked about his symptoms, and named medicines. Bellodi listened with an absent smile.

'D'you hear me,' asked Brescianelli, 'or am I a nuisance?'

'No, no,' protested Bellodi, 'I'm delighted to see you again. By the way, where are you going? ... I'll come with you,' and, without waiting for an answer, took his friend by the arm; with this gesture, one he had almost forgotten, he really did begin to feel the need of company, of talk, of distraction from his anger.

But Brescianelli now began asking him about Sicily; what was it like, how was life down there; and what about its crime?

Bellodi said that Sicily was incredible.

'Yes, indeed; incredible ... I have Sicilian friends too; quite extraordinary people ... And now they have home rule, their own government. The government of the *lupara*, I call it ... Incredible, that's just the word.'

'Italy's incredible, too. You have to go to Sicily to realize just how incredible Italy is.'

'Maybe the whole of Italy is becoming a sort of Sicily. When I read about the scandals of that regional government of theirs, an idea occurred to me. Scientists say that the palm tree line, that is the climate suitable to growth of the palm, is moving north, five hundred metres, I think it was, every year ... The palm tree line ... I call it the coffee line, the strong black coffee line ... It's rising like mercury in a thermometer, this palm tree line, this strong coffee line, this scandal line, rising up throughout Italy and already passed Rome ... ' He broke off suddenly and said to a smiling young woman approaching them: 'You're incredible too: incredibly lovely ... '

'What d'you mean: "too"? Who's the other?'

'Sicily ... Another woman. Mysterious, implacable, vengeful ... and lovely ... like you. Captain Bellodi, whom I have the pleasure of introducing, was telling me about Sicily' – he turned to Bellodi – 'and this is Livia, Livia Giannelli, whom you may remember as a girl: now she's a woman and won't have anything to do with me.'

'Have you come from Sicily?' asked Livia.

'Yes,' said Brescianelli, 'he's down there as a "filthy policeman", as they say,' imitating the cavernous voice and Catanese accent of Angelo Musco.

'I adore Sicily,' said Livia, moving between them and taking their arms.

'This is Parma,' thought Bellodi in sudden happiness,

117

'and this is a girl from Parma. You're home, and to hell with Sicily.'

But Livia wanted to hear the incredible facts about incredible Sicily: 'I've been to Taormina once; and to Syracuse for the Greek plays, but they tell me that really to know Sicily one must go into the interior ... Where are you stationed?'

Bellodi gave the name of the town; neither Livia nor Brescianelli had ever heard of it.

'What's it like?' asked the girl.

'An old town with plaster-walled houses, steep streets and flights of steps, and, at the top of every street and flight of steps, an ugly church.'

'And the men; are the men very jealous?'

'After their own fashion.'

'And the mafia, what's this mafia the papers are always going on about?'

'Yes, what *is* the mafia?' urged Brescianelli.

'It's very complicated to explain,' said Bellodi, 'it's just incredible.'

Biting sleet was beginning to fall, and a white sky foretold heavy snow. Livia suggested they go home with her: some of her women friends were coming and they could listen to some splendid old jazz records, records unearthed by a miracle; there'd also be some good Scotch whisky and Carlos Primero brandy. 'And food?' asked Brescianelli. Livia promised that there would be food too.

They found Livia's sister and two other girls stretched out on the hearth rug in front of a blazing fire, glasses beside them, and the haunting rhythm of 'Funeral at the Vieux Colombier, New Orleans', on a record-player.

They adored Sicily too. The knives which, according to them, were flashed in jealousy, gave them delicious tremors. Sicilian women they pitied, but also envied a little. The red of blood became the red of the painter Guttuso. Picasso's cock on the cover of Brancati's Bell' Antonio', they said, was a charming emblem for Sicily. The thought of the mafia gave them more tremors: and they asked for explanations, stories of the terrible deeds the captain must have seen.

Bellodi told the story of a medical officer in a Sicilian prison who took it into his head, quite rightly, to remove from the mafia convicts the privilege of residing permanently in the prison hospital. The prison was full of genuine sick cases, even some tubercular ones, living in cells and common dormitories, while these mafia chiefs, bursting with health, occupied the sick-bay in order to enjoy better treatment. The doctor gave instructions for them to be sent back to their ordinary quarters and for the sick to be admitted to hospital. The doctor's instructions were disregarded by both warders and governor. The doctor wrote to the Ministry. The next thing that happened was that one night he was summoned to the prison where, he was told, a prisoner had urgent need of him. He went. At one point in the prison he suddenly found himself alone among the convicts; and he was then beaten up with skill and precision by the mafia chiefs. The warders noticed nothing. The doctor reported the attack to the Public Prosecutor and the Ministry, on which some, not all, of the ringleaders were transferred to another prison. Next, the Ministry relieved the doctor of his post on the grounds that his zeal had given rise to incidents. Being a member of a left-wing party, he applied to it for support, but was told that it was better to let things slide. Unable to obtain redress in any other way he then applied to a mafia leader, who did at least give him the satisfaction of having one of his assailants beaten up in the prison to which he had been transferred. The culprit, he was assured, had been given a thorough working-over.

This episode the girls found quite delightful. Brescianelli was horrified.

Sandwiches were made. They ate, drank whisky and brandy and listened to jazz. Then they talked about Sicily again, then about love, then about sex. Bellodi felt like a convalescent: highly sensitive, susceptible, famished. 'To hell with Sicily! To hell with it all!'

He went home at about midnight, crossing the whole city on foot. Parma lay bewitched under snow, silent, deserted ... 'In Sicily it doesn't often snow,' he thought, 'and perhaps a civilization's character is conditioned by snow or sun, according to which is more prevalent.' He felt a little fuzzy in the head. But before reaching home he knew, with utter lucidity, that he loved Sicily and was going back.

'Even if it's the end of me,' he said aloud.

TAILPIECE BY THE AUTHOR

'Excuse the length of this letter,' wrote a Frenchman or Frenchwoman of that great eighteenth century of theirs, 'but I have had no time to make it shorter.' I cannot make this excuse with regard to the golden rule that even a short story should be shortened. I took a whole year, from one summer to the next, to shorten this one, not working at it constantly of course, but side by side with quite other activities and preoccupations. What I hoped to achieve by pruning was not so much proportion, stripped essence and rhythm, as self-defence against the possible reactions of any who might consider themselves more or less directly attacked in it. In Italy, as is well-known, some things must not be made light of, so think what happens when one takes them seriously. In books and films the United States of America can have imbecile generals, corrupt judges and crooked police. So can England, France (at least up till the present), Sweden and so on. Italy has never had, has not and never will have them. That's how it is and, as Giusti said of those ambassadors whom Barnabo Visconti forced to swallow signet, parchment and seal, a fuss ought to be made about it. I don't feel heroic enough to face charges of libel and slander, not deliberately at any rate. So, when I realized that my imagination had not given due consideration to the limits imposed by the laws of the State and, more than by the laws, by the susceptibilities of those whose duty it is to enforce them,

I began to prune and prune. In the first and second drafts the thread of the story has remained substantially unchanged: some characters have disappeared, others become anonymous, a sequence or two omitted. Maybe, even, the story has gained. One thing is certain, however: I was unable to write it with that complete freedom to which every writer is entitled (and I call myself a writer only because I happen to put pen to paper).

Needless to say, there is no character or event in this book which bears anything but a fortuitous resemblance to any real person or actual occurrence.

THE MORO AFFAIR

Extended edition with a new foreword

On 16 March 1978 Aldo Moro, a former Prime Minister of Italy, was ambushed in Rome. Within three minutes the gang killed all five members of his escort and bundled Moro into one of three getaway cars. An hour later the Red Brigades announced that Moro was in their hands; on March 18 they said he would be tried in a 'people's court of justice'. Seven weeks later Moro's body was discovered in the boot of a Renault parked in the crowded centre of Rome.

'The greatest compliment one can pay this fascinating book is to say that it reads like a fable about power anywhere in the world' *Independent*

'The Moro affair, the political crime, will not be forgotten; also, thanks to Sciascia, the tragic events have gained universal dimension. He has convinced us that real tragedies still happen, and that there is always further need of further criticism of our understanding and practice of power' *Irish Times*

SICILIAN UNCLES

Leonardo Sciascia

'The best evocation of Sicily I've read, this is one for crime connoisseurs' Leslie Forbes, *Daily Mail*

'In ordinary detective stories there is always a good deal of disposable material, standard wrapping produced by the simple necessity of having things happen somewhere. There is nothing of the kind in Sciascia' Frank Kermode

A Sicilian uncle is a mentor, a patron, but a sinister and treacherous one. This quartet of thriller novellas shows illusions being lost and ideals betrayed amid war and revolution. They are set at turning points of modern history: the revolutions of 1848; the Spanish Civil War; the Allied invasion of Sicily in 1943; and the death of Stalin ten years later. Each story is full of vivid characters and is like a door opening onto history. This is entertaining writing of a very high order.

THE WINE-DARK SEA
Leonardo Sciascia

'One of the major writers of the age' *Times Literary Supplement*

Here are some of Leonardo Sciascia's greatest stories, brief and haunting: the realist tradition at its best. In one tale a couple of men talk, cynically yet earnestly, about the etymology of the word 'mafia'. The reader comes to realize that he is eavesdropping on the musings of a mafia boss and his underling. In another story a group of peasants are taken on board ship and promised that they will be put ashore illegally at Trenton, New Jersey. After a long time at sea, their landfall is far from what they expected.

EQUAL DANGER

District Attorney Varga is shot dead. Then Judge Sanza is killed. Then Judge Azar. Are these random murders, or part of a conspiracy? Inspector Rogas thinks he might know, but as soon as he makes progress he is transferred and encouraged to pin the crimes on the Left. But how committed are the cynical, fashionable, comfortable revolutionaries to revolution – or anything? Who is doing what to whom? This is one of Sciascia's best political thrillers.

'The master of sophisticated detective fiction' *Guardian*

'Only very rarely can we say of such works [crime novels] that they look at questions of social justice with the informed eye of the intelligent artist. We can, however, make that claim for the stories of Leonardo Sciascia' Frank Kermode

'The best evocation of the mafia in its birthplace in Sicily' *Evening Standard*